Fast

Pitch

By

Graysen Morgen

2013

Fast Pitch © 2013 Graysen Morgen

Triplicity Publishing, LLC

ISBN-13: 978-0988619623

ISBN-10: 0988619628

All rights reserved. No part of this publication may be reproduced, distributed, or transmitted in any form without permission.

This is a work of fiction. Names, characters, places, and incidents are the product of the author's imagination and are used fictitiously. Any resemblance to actual persons, living or dead, business establishments, events of any kind, or locales is entirely coincidental.

Printed in the United States of America

First Edition – 2013

Cover Design: Triplicity Publishing, LLC

Interior Design: Triplicity Publishing, LLC

Also by Graysen Morgen

Acknowledgements

Special thanks to Lee Fitzsimmons, the person who spends countless hours correcting my mistakes. You are right, it is hard to find good help! Also, a big thanks to my mate, CJ, and her eagle eyes!

Dedication

This book is dedicated to my partner. After years of asking me to write a softball book, here you go. Without you none of this would be possible and I thank you for it every day.

Chapter 1

"Are you ready yet? We were supposed to have be there five minutes ago, Dash." Graham Cahill ran a hand through her spiky, short, dirty-blond hair as she paced the floor of their tiny campus apartment. She was a senior at the University of Central Oregon, studying biology, and was also the catcher on the softball team and the team captain.

Her roommate, teammate, and best friend, Dashtin Oliver, swayed across the living room floor with a goofy grin on her face, pulling her plain brown hair back into a ponytail. She was the shortstop on the team and also a senior.

"Don't get all bent out of shape, Graham. It's the first day of practice and it's snowing. I seriously doubt we'll be doing a whole lot."

"I'm leaving. If you're not in the Jeep in the next few seconds you can walk," Graham said, grabbing her bag and hustling out the door.

The red Jeep Wrangler was rolling backwards as Dashtin jumped in with her bag. Her car was in the shop for the umpteenth time so she was relying on Graham for transportation and Graham was punctual whereas Dashtin was notorious for being late.

"You're a pain in the ass," Graham said.

"Yeah, but you love me." Dashtin smacked her arm. Graham rolled her eyes and shifted gears.

"You know, you may have been on time this morning if you hadn't had to chase your latest conquest out of your bed."

"How was I to know the girl would be so difficult to wake up?" Dashtin said.

"Do you even know her name?"

"Does it matter?"

Graham shook her head. She cared for her best friend and worried about her. In the four years that she'd known her, Dashtin had never had a serious girlfriend. She preferred the one night stand routine, claiming she was too young to settle down and play house.

The Jeep brushed up against the snow bank as Graham parked in the lot outside of the athletic building. Both women grabbed their bags and hurried inside.

~

Linda Walker, the head coach of the UCO Pioneer softball team, was going over the team rules as her two star players meandered in.

"What's rule number one, ladies?" she asked.

"Don't be late," they said simultaneously.

"What happens when we are late?" Coach Walker asked.

Graham and Dashtin pushed their bags to the side. "We assume the position," they said as they got down on the floor in the push-up position.

"So where were we before our fearless captain and her sidekick decided to greet us with their presence?" she said, checking her notes. "Oh yes, as you can see it's not a good idea to be late to team functions. I take my job seriously and I take this team seriously. Those of you who think that this is playtime will learn very quickly that you are wrong." She talked for another five minutes before she allowed the two to join the rest of the team.

Graham's arms were burning. She wanted to bitch-slap her best friend.

"Now that we're all together, let me start by introducing our two new team members. Claudia Manning comes to us from Seattle, Washington. She's an outfielder with a three-forty batting average." Coach Walker pointed to her and a light skinned black girl stood up, smiling nervously.

When she sat down the coach pointed to another girl who stood. Graham noticed how petite the girl was right away. She had dark, wavy hair pulled back in a ponytail, bright green eyes that glowed like cat eyes, and a silky smooth olive complexion.

"This is our new pitcher, Bailey Michaels. She was an All-Conference player for her high school in Austin, Texas with a three year record of striking out 102 batters in 51 innings."

Bailey smiled and sat back down. Dashtin elbowed Graham and held her hand out at dwarf height when she looked at her. Graham grinned and rolled her eyes.

"I'd like to be the first to welcome you both to the Pioneers," Coach Walker said. "I know you haven't had a chance to meet everyone yet, but let me introduce my coaching staff." She pointed to a wiry redhead who waved. "This is Deanna Parker, the pitching and assistant coach. Bailey you will get to know her very well."

Coach Walker pointed to the young woman next to her. She had dark, straight hair pulled back in a ponytail and dark brown eyes. "This is Helena Mendez, our student coach for this season. Now that we all know each other let's break-up into groups. If we can't be out on the field then we'll work out in the gym."

Everyone moved quickly from the locker room into the large gym full of weight training equipment with a few treadmills and elliptical machines. Graham and Dashtin walked over to one of the weight benches and started stacking weights on the bar.

"What do you think of the new pitcher?" Dashtin asked.

"I have no idea. I don't know her."

"She looks too small to be a pitcher. She's cute though."

"I can't tell you anything about her until I see her throw a ball. She is a little shorter than most pitchers and for crying out loud don't sleep with her. She's a freshman," Graham said, lying down on the bench. She pushed the bar up off the stand with Dashtin's guidance and lowered the weight to her chest before pushing it up.

"Oh it's not me she's interested in," Dashtin said when she saw the younger pitcher watching Graham lift the weights.

"What?" Graham said, wiping the sweat from her forehead.

"Nothing." Dashtin raised an eyebrow protectively at the young pitcher when their eyes connected.

They quickly switched positions and Dashtin went to work bench-pressing the weight. Graham looked around the room and noticed Bailey on the rowing machine. Every time she moved, her T-shirt rode up slightly showing off her six pack abs and her arms flexed with every pull of the machine. Graham took a second look. The young girl might be short in stature, but she had a hard-body under her workout clothes.

Two hours later, they had worked their way around to all of the different weight stations and ran on the treadmills.

"Practice is officially over ladies," Coach Walker said. "Tomorrow we'll hit the indoor cages if the snow hasn't cleared outside."

"Graham, I need a few minutes," Coach Parker said when Graham and Dashtin started for the locker room. She called the new pitcher over to where they were standing. "Bailey have you met our catcher and team captain, Graham Cahill?"

"No," Bailey stuck her hand out. Graham wrapped her hand around the smaller, soft hand and shook it gently. She smiled down at the bright green eyes connecting with her blue ones.

"You two need to get to know each other. You'll be attached at the hip. We'll start drills tomorrow," Coach Parker said.

"So, you're my catcher." Bailey said with a grin, rolling her bottom lip between her teeth.

"I'm the team catcher. Pitchers come and go but I'm there from the first pitch to the last, every game," Graham said.

"Looks like we have a lot in common then."

"Are you really the stand-out pitcher that coach says you are?" Graham asked. She had to admit the girl was very cute, but very young and very cocky.

"You don't think I am." Bailey asked.

"I didn't say that."

"It's implied."

"How tall are you?" Graham asked.

"Five-foot-two," Bailey rolled her eyes and looked up at Graham who was clearly four or five inches taller. She'd been judged over her height her entire softball career. Her first coach had said there was no way she'd ever be a college level pitcher. She planned to prove everyone wrong.

Graham nodded and turned towards the locker room. Bailey watched her walk away. Graham was leaving with Dashtin on her heels as Bailey entered the locker room.

"Roll through McDonald's on the way home," Dashtin said.

"Yuck. You need to quit eating that shit food."

"I don't see you cooking for me, Ms. Healthy Homemaker."

Chapter 2

Graham was reading an online syllabus for one of her upcoming classes for the spring semester. She was glad to have no classes for a week. Dashtin was down the hallway singing to the blaring radio. Graham popped her head out of her doorway in time to see her strut by with her hair down which only meant one thing, she was going out on the prowl.

"I'm going to *Sister Fred's* with Whitney and Vanessa from the team. A few other people are going to meet us there. You should come with us. Whatever nerdy thing you're in there doing can wait," Dashtin said.

"I'm reading a class syllabus and trying to decide if I really want that class first thing in the morning."

Dashtin raised her eyebrows and smirked.

"If this nerd hadn't done some of your homework freshman year, you probably wouldn't be in your senior year now."

"Touché. Now get dressed. We're leaving in a few minutes. I'm going to call Whitney and tell her I'm riding with you so they can just meet us there."

"I'm surprised Whitney's hanging out with you. Didn't you sleep with her?"

Dashtin laughed. "That was sophomore year, way in the past."

"I see." Graham shook her head and went to her closet in search of something to wear for a night out on the town.

~

Dashtin walked into the restaurant that doubled as a bar with a dance floor. She held Graham's hand, pulling her through the crowd to the back where their teammates and other friends already had a high-top table.

"You guys seem to be late a lot lately. What gives?" Whitney asked. She was the first base player on the team and had long, thick curly auburn hair. Graham and Dashtin pointed at each other and laughed.

"This morning was her fault," Graham said, pointing at her best friend.

"I take it tonight was yours?" Whitney asked her.

"Something like that."

Dashtin grabbed two fresh glasses for the pitcher sitting on the table. She filled both glasses with the light beer and handed one to Graham.

Graham studied the menu while Dashtin watched the people dancing nearby.

"What are they doing here?" Dashtin said.

"Who?" Graham looked up in time to see the two new freshmen from the team walking from the dance floor towards their table. She watched them take seats at the opposite end. Bailey's eyes met hers briefly before she turned back to the menu.

"What's your grudge with the newbie's?" Whitney asked. "Did they turn you down?"

"Funny," Dashtin said, rolling her eyes.

"The pitcher's a little cocky," Graham said.

"I don't know much about them except they're in the East Dorm with Katie and Hannah."

"I was in the East Dorm my freshman year. In fact, that's where I met Graham before we even had our first team meeting. I had no idea who she was," Dashtin said.

"Did she hit on you?" Whitney asked Graham.

"Of course. She hits on everyone." Graham laughed. "Honestly, I'm not her type so it worked out for the better and we became really good friends right away."

Graham looked towards the end of the table. "I wonder if they're as overwhelmed as I was."

Dashtin followed her line of sight. "They've been here for six months. I'm sure they're fine."

When the waitress walked by their table, Graham ordered a cheeseburger and fries and took a sip of her beer. She watched the enigmatic pitcher placing her order.

"Hey, bump-on-a-log, let's dance," Dashtin said, nudging shoulders with her.

Graham stood and held her hand out to Dashtin.

"So chivalrous." Dashtin grinned, pretending to swoon.

"Oh get over yourself." Graham laughed.

Graham and Dashtin danced to a handful of fast song with smiles on their faces. Anyone that knew them knew that they weren't together, but a few of their moves made them look like a lot more than friends.

"How long have they been together?" Claudia, one of the new freshmen, asked.

"They've been inseparable since their freshman year. They're not a couple though, actually never have been. They're just best friends," Vanessa said.

Bailey watched the dance floor.

The music quickly changed to a slower song so they walked back to the table hand-in-hand, laughing and smiling. Graham sat down, drank a few sips of her beer, and dug right into the cheeseburger.

An hour later, Graham still had part of her first beer in her glass and Dashtin was dancing with multiple girls on the dance floor. Helena Mendez, the team's student coach, made her way over to the table where Graham was sitting.

"Hey," Graham said.

"Want to dance?" Helena asked.

"No thanks."

"You don't know what you're missing," Helena bent down and whispered close to her ear.

"Thanks, but no thanks," Graham stated more firmly. She was ready to go anyway and she knew Dashtin would find a ride home with no problem so she tossed some cash on the table and stood up. Helena quickly walked away.

"Don't drink too much tonight, ladies, especially if you're driving. I'm sure Coach Walker will be out for blood tomorrow and we don't need to be hung over," Graham said to the group.

"Yes, ma'am, fearless leader." Whitney saluted.

Graham laughed and shook her head.

"Hey Graham, if you're leaving would you mind running Bailey and Claudia back to the East Dorm? I'm not sure how much longer I will be and they have a curfew," Vanessa said.

"Sure," Graham said, waving for them to join her.

A light sheen of snow was falling when they got outside. Graham unlocked the Jeep and Claudia climbed into the backseat while Bailey sat in the front passenger seat.

"How do you girls like East Dorm?"Graham said as she drove out of the parking lot towards campus.

"It's okay," Claudia said.

"I was in there my freshman year too. I don't think much has changed."

"Where do you live?" Bailey asked.

"University Pointe Apartments."

"Do you have roommates?" Bailey asked.

"Dashtin and I share an apartment."

"That figures," Bailey said under her breath. She focused her attention on the passing buildings as Graham drove through the middle of the college campus to get to the dorms on the other side. The freshmen were housed as far away from the bars as possible.

"What's your major?" Claudia asked.

"Biology," Graham said. "Have you two decided on majors yet?"

"No. I can't decide between business and education," Claudia said. "My mom's a teacher and I've always wanted to be a teacher, but I like the idea of working in the corporate world one day too. What made you pick biology?"

"I've always been into science. I'm a closet nerd." She laughed and looked over at Bailey.

"What about you?"

"What about me?" Bailey asked, turning away from the window to look at her.

Their eyes met in the dark. The streetlights glowing through the windshield lit up Bailey's face. She had the most beautiful, soulful eyes Graham had ever seen.

Graham's breath caught in her throat causing her to start coughing. She parked at the curb in front of the dorm building and was more than happy to see the freshmen depart her vehicle. She quickly drove away once they were inside the building.

Chapter 3

Sunday morning, Graham and Dashtin walked into practice a few minutes early. They were both wearing the blue and black colored team warm-ups like everyone else in the room. There was still snow on the ground which meant they would be using the indoor facilities for the day's practice. Graham took a seat next to Whitney who was visibly nursing a hangover. She bumped shoulders with her and shook her head. Dashtin also had a hangover, but Graham was probably the only one who noticed.

"Good morning, ladies," Coach Walker said loudly as she entered the room. "Let's split up into groups and hit the batting cages since the snow's not going to give us a break today."

Coach Parker pulled Graham, the back-up catcher, and the three pitchers aside and led them over to the pitching cages which were around the corner from the batting cages and separated by a wall.

"Pair off. Graham, you work with Bailey," she said.

Graham nodded and went to work putting on her catcher's gear. She wasn't taking any chances. When she was ready, Graham took her position at the halfway point between the mound and home plate so she could toss the ball back and forth with Bailey while she slowly loosened her arm. She adjusted her position further back as the young pitcher got warmer.

Graham caught the ball and walked towards Bailey. "Has Coach Parker gone over the hand signals with you?"

"No."

"I call the games from the plate so you need to watch me. I'll email you the signals so you can learn them. For now, I'll just call the pitches out," Graham said. She walked to the plate and waited for Bailey to settle in at the pitching rubber before squatting into her catching position.

"Let's start with a rise ball," Graham yelled down to her.

Bailey released a wild pitch that Graham had to dive for. After the fifth or sixth time that she'd had to dive for the ball, Graham called another pitch, then another until they'd gone through all of the pitches. Well over fifty-percent of the pitches that Bailey had thrown were wild. Graham was literally worn out when she stood up and walked over to Bailey.

"Are you nervous?" she asked.

"No," Bailey said casually.

"What's with all of the wild balls?"

"I'm an aggressive pitcher."

"Aggressive pitching and wild crazy pitching are two totally different things," Graham said.

"Everyone is entitled to their own opinion," Bailey countered.

"You can't go into a game throwing the ball like that. You need to get some control."

"What's going on?" Coach Parker asked, walking up to them. The student coach, Helena Mendez, was with her.

"Ask your star pitcher here," Graham growled.

Bailey crossed her arms and raised an eyebrow. "She doesn't like the way I pitch."

"You throw wild crazy balls all over the damn place. How am I supposed to catch them?" Graham said.

Bailey shrugged.

"Okay, okay. Calm down. Graham you need to work with her on ball control. You two need to be in sync and know each other's moves before they're made. Starting tomorrow I want you both in here alone an hour a day. Put your schedules together and figure it out. Work on one pitch and catch at a time until you get it right. I'll check in with you mid-week," Coach Parker said.

"Are you kidding me?" Graham said, taking off her catching gear.

"No, I'm not kidding you. She's the starting pitcher for this season and you're the catcher so the two of you have got to learn to work together. Spend some time off the field and get to know each other and maybe you won't be so hostile towards each other."

"I didn't do anything," Bailey said.

"I saw some of those pitches and Assistant Coach Mendez watched your session. She pointed out the aggression between you two. Graham knows what she's talking about. Listen to her," Coach Parker said. "Both of you need to go hit the batting cages for a half hour then you can go. Maybe that'll help you work off some of the negative energy between you."

Graham tossed her gear to the side and jogged over to the empty batting cages. The rest of the team had been dismissed for the day. Bailey followed, choosing the cage next to hers. Since she was left-handed and Graham was right, this meant they'd be facing each other.

"It'll get better," Helena said to her.

"Yeah, you think she's so great you try catching her pitches," Graham growled.

"I wasn't talking about her. I was talking about you."

Graham ignored her and stepped back taking the first pitch. She settled back in the box swinging with everything she had at the second ball. The crack of the bat was so loud, Bailey stepped over the plate and was nearly hit by the pitch coming at her. Graham focused all of her anger hitting pitch after pitch until she was too tired to hold the bat.

Coach Parker stood to the side watching them. If they could just learn to contain the fire burning between them they'd be an unstoppable combo. She couldn't blame Graham for being mad. Bailey was one of the best high school pitchers in the country, based on her record, but she was a wild pitcher, something catchers hated.

"Alright, let's call it a day, ladies. And so there's no hard feelings, Graham, I'd like you to give Bailey a ride home."

Graham bit her tongue, gritted her teeth, and nodded. "Come on, I don't have all day," she said to Bailey as soon as the coach was out of earshot.

"I didn't ask you to drive me anywhere," Bailey said, rushing to keep up with the taller woman.

"I didn't say you did."

"I have a car," Bailey said, climbing into the Jeep.

"Then why aren't you driving it?"

"When I was home for the holidays my little brother borrowed it and wrecked it. He's only sixteen."

"Sounds like you don't have one anymore."

"You don't like me much, do you?" Bailey asked.

Graham slammed on the brakes a little hard and pulled into a parking space at the East Dorm building.

"Bailey, I never said I didn't like you. What I don't like is cocky, know-it-all freshmen and wild pitchers. You're turning out to be all three."

Bailey shrugged and got out. "I guess I'll see you tomorrow. What time are we meeting?"

"I'm free in the afternoons this week. I can meet you at two. Does that work for you?"

"See you at two then," Bailey said, shutting the door.

~

"What happened to you?" Dashtin asked when Graham walked in. She was laying on the couch, watching TV, while tossing M&M's into the air and catching them in her mouth.

"You're going to choke doing that," Graham said, walking by her. She went down the hall to her room and stripped to go take a shower.

"When Coach Walker let us go, I checked on you and you guys were still hard at it. Coach Parker must've had her panties in a bunch," Dashtin said from the bathroom doorway.

Graham was already standing under the spray, willing the hot water to wash away the miserable practice.

"It's that new pitcher. She's wild and uncontrollable. My entire body hurts from chasing ball after ball. Coach Parker seems to think I can get her in line. We have daily practice sessions on our own, starting tomorrow."

"That sucks. Why doesn't Coach Parker put her in her place?"

"No shit. I don't know. She's relying on me to get her in line and to make matters worse, Bailey doesn't think she's doing anything wrong. I just want to smack her."

"I'm sure she wants to do a lot more than smack you," Dashtin said, still tossing up and catching the candy in her mouth.

Graham stuck her soapy head out of the curtain. "What are you talking about?"

"Have you seen the way she looks at you?"

"Oh please, you think everyone is lusting after everyone." Graham shook her head and closed the curtain.

"Fine. Don't say I didn't warn you when she jumps your body at one of these secret practices."

"Dash, she's just a kid."

"She's eighteen or nineteen. That's legal the last time I checked."

"Then you go after her. The last thing I want is to sleep with her. At this point, I will be doing good to get through this week without choking her," Graham growled. "Can I please wash my ass in peace? I'm tired, hungry, and pissed at the moment. I don't need you harassing me."

"Excuse me, your highness." Dashtin closed the door and went back to the couch.

Chapter 4

Graham was in the gym using the rowing machine, wearing only a sports bra and her gym shorts, when Bailey arrived. She watched the sweaty muscles in Graham's back move with every stroke of the machine. She waited, quietly watching until Graham had finished. Graham turned around and was surprised to see her standing there and Bailey was surprised to see the nicely sculpted body in front of her. Graham wasn't as flat-chested as she appeared to be with her workout uniform on. She had a nice, small handful of perky round breasts, bunched together under her sports bra.

"I didn't hear you come in," Graham said, wiping the sweat from her face with a towel.

"You looked determined so I didn't want to interrupt you."

"It's easy to get lost in yourself on that machine." Graham put her T-shirt on and walked from the gym to the catching cages with Bailey following her. Her catching equipment was already there so she began putting it on.

"I got the email you sent with the hand signals."

"Good. You will need to learn them as quick as possible."

"I know them."

Graham stopped what she was doing and looked over at Bailey. "You memorized it in one day?"

"It's only four signals for the pitches and then the direction."

"Alright," Graham shrugged. "Let's work on one pitch each day and see how that goes."

"You're the expert."

"Screwball today," Graham yelled, taking her position behind the plate.

The first pitch was wild and Graham fell back on her butt trying to get to it. The next few pitches weren't as bad. When Bailey was on she was a hell of a pitcher, but when she was off she was on the other side of the map. For every dozen great pitches, she threw three or four wild ones. At the end of the hour, Graham was ready for the practice to be over with. Her body hurt once again from stretching at odd angles.

"Better than yesterday," Graham said when they met in the middle. "Tomorrow we'll work on the drop ball. On Friday we will pull it all together and see what we have."

"Fine."

"Bailey, I'm not picking on you. You're a really good pitcher, but we have to get these wild pitches under control."

"I've never had my pitching critiqued and I don't really care for it."

"This is NCAA Division I softball. If you want to be the starting pitcher you'll learn to control your pitches and listen to me. Otherwise, you'll be sitting on the bench watching the game like a spectator," Graham said.

"I don't need you telling me what to do. That's why we have a pitching coach."

Graham picked up her gear and turned to walk away. "Do you need a ride?"

"Nope," Bailey growled, walking in the opposite direction.

Graham shrugged and left her on her own.

~

"How was practice?" Dashtin asked.

Graham blew out a deep breath and flopped on the couch. "She can pitch a ball like no one I've ever seen, then all of a sudden she throws a wild, crazy, out of control ball that I have to dive for. It's like every fifth or sixth pitch just gets away from her. I don't get it."

"How's her attitude?"

"Not much better."

"Is she flirting with you yet?"

"What? No. She probably can't stand me," Graham said. "I see you got your car back."

"Yeah, Whitney took me to get it earlier when they called."

"Good, I'm tired of chauffeuring your ass all over town. I'm going to take a shower," Graham tossed her cell phone on the table with her keys and went to her room. She wasn't gone ten minutes when her phone started ringing over and over. Dashtin noticed it said Whitney so she answered it.

"Why the hell did you make Bailey walk back to the dorm in the cold with snow on the ground?" Whitney said with a little bit of edge in her voice.

"Wait, what are you talking about? This is Dashtin."

"Why are you answering Graham's phone?"

"She's in the shower and it wouldn't stop ringing. What's wrong?"

"Graham apparently just left Bailey to walk back to the dorm in the snow."

"Bailey doesn't have a car or know anyone else with one?" Dashtin said.

"That's not the point."

"Bailey's an adult. She needs to put her big girl pants on."

"Oh grow up, Dashtin. Tell Graham to call me when she gets out," Whitney said before hanging up.

A few minutes later, Graham appeared squeaky clean and freshly dressed.

"Woman, you've stirred the hornets' nest," Dashtin said, shaking her head.

"What are you talking about?"

"Whitney wouldn't stop calling so I answered your phone and boy is she pissed."

"About what?"

"Did you leave Bailey at the field?"

"Yeah. We finished at the pitching cage and she went one way and I went the other. What's wrong?"

"Whitney thinks you left her to walk back to the dorm in the snow."

"What the hell? I asked her if she needed a ride and she said 'nope'. So I left."

"You better call Whitney and tell her that."

"Oh good grief! This girl is going to drive me crazy." Graham grabbed her phone and pushed the button to dial Whitney's number.

"Hey I'm going to the sandwich shop on the corner. You want anything?" Dashtin asked.

"Yeah, get me a turkey club with swiss," Graham said as she waited for Whitney to pick up.

"What's going on?" Graham said when Whitney answered.

"Why did you leave Bailey to walk in the snow?"

"Whitney, I have no idea who told you that, but I asked her after practice is she needed a ride and she said no so I left. I'm not her babysitter."

"Claudia just told Vanessa that she walked back to the dorm from practice."

"Well, maybe you should ask Bailey why she walked instead of jumping to conclusions about me. I'm not an asshole, Whitney."

"She's really struggling with this whole pitching thing. Maybe you should hang out with her away from softball."

"Is she a freshman in high school or a freshman in college? You sound like Coach Parker." Graham sighed. "I'll talk to her."

~

The next two days of practice went virtually the same as the first. Graham was trying not to get frustrated.

She was learning how to handle the wild pitches and Bailey was quickly learning the pitching signals perfectly even though she still threw whatever she wanted. Graham knew the pressure was getting to both of them and that would only lead to another argument unless they got away from the game.

"Do you want to go get some dinner tonight?" Graham asked when their session ended.

"Are you asking me out?" Bailey raised an eyebrow.

"What?! No. I just thought maybe you'd want to get away from the softball scene for a little bit. Coach Parker seems to think it will help us communicate if we get to know each other away from the field."

Bailey laughed. "I was only teasing you. I know you're taken. I guess we can hang out if you don't harp on my pitching the entire time." She stuffed her glove in her locker and turned around to see Graham sitting in a chair watching her.

"First of all, I'm single so I have no idea who told you I wasn't and second, I don't want to hear the word softball for the rest of the night so I think we agree on that."

"I'll be ready around six-thirty," Bailey said.

"I'll pick you up. I wouldn't want you to walk in the snow," Graham teased.

"I never said you made me walk in the snow. I was pissed and wanted to walk. Claudia just assumed something and spread it around like wildfire. I'm grown. I don't need to be babysat."

"Good because I'm not a babysitter. Now, do you need a ride to the dorm?"

Bailey laughed. "No, Alex is picking me up."

~

Graham ran a few errands and checked in with her advisor about changing the time of her molecular chemistry class before heading home. Dashtin was passed out on the couch when she walked in. Graham shook her head and went to her room. She was already working on her senior thesis and if she planned to get into the graduate program for her masters after graduation in the summer then she needed to work harder than ever before.

An hour later, she took a quick shower and walked out of her room, dressed in jeans and a gray sweater with a black T-shirt under it. She looked like she was going out.

"Why didn't you wake me when you got home?" Dashtin said.

"I'm not your alarm clock," Graham chided.

"You look like you have a hot date."

"What if I do?"

"Get the hell out. I can't remember the last time you had a date." Dashtin laughed.

"That's because the entire town thinks you and I are together."

Dashtin guffawed. "If they only knew. That'll never happen. Seriously, what's up?"

"I'm going to dinner with Bailey."

"As in a date?"

"No. Nothing like that. I'm thinking that maybe taking our minds off the rift between us on the field might help the situation."

"Don't sleep with her," Dashtin said.

"Really, Dash? That's your M.O. not mine."

"Where are you going?"

"I don't know. Maybe *Sister Fred's*."

"Have fun. She can't even drink. That's going to be a bore."

Graham laughed. "Don't wait up."

"She has a curfew."

"God, she's young." Graham shook her head and grabbed her keys.

Chapter 5

Graham knew the menu by heart, but read it again anyway. She was nervous and that was something she wasn't used to. The young woman sitting across from her intrigued her and annoyed her at the same time, but most of the time she downright drove her crazy.

A few people came over to their table to say hey to Graham.

"You're popular," Bailey said.

Graham peered over the top of her menu. Bailey's dark hair was hanging in loose waves just passed her shoulders. When it fell across her forehead she casually pushed it back off of her face in a move that sent chills up Graham's spine. She'd never seen the young pitcher with her hair down. She's was beautiful.

"Are you okay?" Bailey asked.

"What? Yeah. Sorry I...did you ask me something?" Graham mentally chided herself for staring at the young woman and sniffing the air like a dog but she was sure the floral scent tickling her nose was coming from across the table.

"I said you're popular."

"Me? No. I know most of these people through Dashtin. She knows the entire town."

"I'm surprised she didn't come with you."

"She was glued to the TV when I left. She's into some new show and recorded a bunch of reruns to get caught up."

They both ordered dinner when the waitress appeared.

"You can drink if you want. I don't mind," Bailey said.

Graham smiled. "I'm not a big drinker."

"What are you going to do after graduation?" Bailey asked, changing the subject.

"Going to graduate school, I hope."

"What does a biologist do? I mean I know some people go on to become doctors and other things."

"Are you asking what I want to be when I grow up?" Graham laughed. "I want to be a microbiologist. Basically, you sit in a lab all day doing research and experiments trying to cure diseases."

"Wow, that's big. It must be something if you're that passionate about it."

"It has to be. Otherwise it would be the most boring job in the world." Graham grinned. "What about you? Do you have a major yet?"

"At the moment it's business administration."

"Are you thinking of changing it?"

"I don't know." Bailey shrugged.

"What did you want to be when you were a kid?"

34

Bailey bit her lower lip casually and looked up. "A taxidermist," she said.

Graham had just taken a sip of her water and had to swallow awkwardly to keep from spewing it all over Bailey.

"What? I'm from Texas. We like animals in the south and taxidermy is huge." Bailey's southern drawl was more noticeable when she talked about home.

"I see," Graham stated.

"Where are you from?"

"Portland."

"What made you stay in-state?"

"I looked at a lot of different schools and was accepted to at least half a dozen, but I had an in-state academic scholarship so I planned to stay in Oregon. Coach Walker needed a catcher so it worked out. How did you wind up in Oregon?"

"All of the big schools in the south wanted to make me an outfielder because of my height. No one thought I could make it as a college level pitcher, well except Coach Walker," Bailey said.

"I think you're a hell of a pitcher, Bailey. You just need to work on ball control."

"I thought we weren't going to talk about softball?" Bailey teased.

Graham smiled and shrugged.

"Let's dance," Bailey said.

"I'm not much of a dancer," Graham said.

Bailey was about to comment when her cell phone beeped. She answered the text and then answered two more after that. By the time their food appeared she had forgotten about dancing.

"So we don't see many people from Texas up here. In fact, I think you're the first one I've met," Graham said between bites.

Bailey grinned. "What's wrong with Texas girls?"

"Nothing. It does explain a few things though. Isn't the state motto 'everything's bigger in Texas?'"

"That and 'don't mess with Texas.' So what do you mean about it explains a few things?"

"You're this little person with this huge personality and attitude. It makes sense that you're from Texas." Graham smiled.

Bailey raised an eyebrow. "That sounds like a compliment and an insult."

"It's neither. Just a comment. Don't take everything so directly," Graham said, pushing her empty plate to the side.

"Yes, ma'am, Coach Cahill."

Graham shook her head and smiled. She tossed some cash on the table and stood when she saw Helena Mendez walking in their direction. "Come on, let's get out of here."

"Leaving so soon, Graham?" Helena said.

"Yeah, I have a busy day tomorrow."

"I was hoping for that dance."

"Not tonight."

"Make sure you get Bailey back to the dorm before curfew," Helena smirked.

"Will do," Graham said over her shoulder as she ushered Bailey through the crowd.

"What's her deal?" Bailey said once they got outside.

"I have no idea. She's been acting strange around me since the first team meeting before you freshmen got here." Graham unlocked the doors to the Jeep and opened Bailey's door for her before walking around to the driver's side.

"It looks like the snow has finally stopped," Bailey said as they drove across campus.

"Yeah, hopefully it stays that way for our first game this weekend." Graham looked over at Bailey. "Are you nervous?"

"I'm not going to lie to you. I have a lot weighing on my shoulders so yes, I'm nervous."

Graham parked in the dorm lot and cut the engine.

"Bailey, you don't need to worry about what people think or say just go out there and pitch the ball. I'll be right there with you along with the rest of the team. There are no individuals. We do everything as a team. Besides, I'll be calling the game so you will have to rely on my skills and trust me at the plate. If all else fails picture the batter naked."

"Like that's going to help." Bailey laughed.

Graham shrugged. "I'll see you tomorrow at practice."

"I had a nice time tonight, Graham. Thanks." As Bailey got out her cell phone rang and she answered it before closing the door.

"Alex, I said I would call you when I got home. I'm literally in the parking lot," Bailey rolled her eyes and smiled at Graham before waving and shutting the door.

~

Graham walked into the apartment and Dashtin was still sitting in front of the TV.

"How was your date?"

"It wasn't a date. We actually had a nice time until Helena appeared."

"Why don't you just hook-up with Helena? She's obviously interested." Dashtin paused the TV show.

"I don't hook-up with people, Dash. You do." Graham tossed her keys on the table and flopped down on the couch next to her. "Why don't you hook-up with her?"

"She's into you not me."

"Yeah well she needs to get over it."

"What did Bailey say about it?"

Graham shrugged. "I don't think she even noticed. She's straight anyway."

"What makes you think she's straight?"

"I'm pretty sure the Alex she was arguing with on the phone is her boyfriend," Graham said.

"Weird."

"How is that weird? You think everyone's a lesbian."

Dashtin laughed. "They are. They just don't know it yet."

"Uh huh and let me guess it's your quest to help them see the rainbow light at the end of the tunnel?" Graham shook her head.

"Something like that," Dashtin laughed.

Graham rose from the couch, stretching the muscles in her back. She kicked her shoes off and turned towards the hallway.

"Is your pitcher ready for this weekend?"

"She's nervous, but as long as she controls the damn ball she'll do fine," Graham said, walking down the hall towards her room.

Chapter 6

The weather held for the first game of the season and opening weekend. Graham was excited to be back on the field. She wore her number seventeen, light blue and black uniform with pride. Dashtin stood in the shortstop position sporting the lucky number thirteen on her back with her long hair up in a ponytail and Bailey graced the pitcher's mound in her double-zero jersey with her dark hair pulled back in a ponytail with a light blue ribbon and a smile on her face.

The first inning went off without a hitch, three up and three down. Then, Whitney hit an RBI in the second inning to push the Pioneers ahead by one. The third and fourth innings were ended quickly with pop ups from both teams. In the fifth, Bailey threw two crazy balls that loaded the bases and allowed the tying run to come in after visibly arguing with Graham over which pitch to throw. Graham immediately ran out to the mound.

"What's going on?" she asked. "You're not throwing what I'm calling. What's the problem?"

"I disagreed with your call," Bailey huffed.

Dashtin ran up to both of them.

"What's the damn problem?"

"We're having a little issue with the pitch calling," Graham said.

"If I disagree with you then I'm going to throw what I want," Bailey said.

"You need to get it together, kid. Graham calls the plays whether you like it or not," Dashtin growled.

"Great," Graham said when she saw Coach Parker walking towards them. Dashtin ran back to her position.

"What's up, ladies?"

"We've got it, coach," Graham said.

"Bailey, open your hand so your palm is facing the sky on the curve. That should give you more control," Coach Parker said before walking back to the dugout.

"We'll lay off the curve until you get it under control," Graham said.

"You need to get your girlfriend under control. I'm not a fucking kid, she's not my boss, and you're not my coach," Bailey sneered before going back to the mound.

Graham raised an eyebrow and jogged back to plate.

The Pioneers were able to get through the fifth and six without using the curve ball and one of the outfielders hit a home run in the seventh winning the game for them.

The team met in the locker room to discuss the game afterwards which was their usual custom. All of the coaches walked in together and stood in the front of the room near the dry erase board with all of the notes and plays written on it.

"First let me say it's nice to get a win in our opening game although it was extremely sloppy. Was the outfield slippery or were we just struggling to get under the ball?

And that mess at the pitching mound better never happen again. Graham, you and Bailey need to figure out how to work together. I thought you've been working on that all week?" She raised her hand when Graham tried to comment. "I think you should all go home and think about this game, what went wrong, and areas you can personally improve so that we don't look like fools again tomorrow. This is our house! We should never play this bad in our house, ladies! Win or not we looked horrible tonight." She slammed her clipboard on the chair. "You're dismissed."

"Graham and Bailey, I need to see you both before you go," Coach Parker said.

Graham put her equipment in her locker and slammed the door. Her uniform was sweaty and itchy and she was ready to go home. The last thing she wanted was another ass-chewing.

"What the hell happened out there tonight?" Coach Parker asked.

"We had a minor disagreement," Graham said.

Bailey sat with her arms crossed.

"What's your side of the story?" Coach Parker asked her.

"I disagreed with the pitches she was calling."

"So let me guess, you threw what you wanted and that's why it went crazy."

"Something like that," Graham said.

"Bailey, you were brought to this team because you have mad pitching skills, but they aren't perfect. If Graham notices something, whether it's with the batter or your pitching, she's going to change things up and you need to be prepared for that. We can't have the two of you arguing at the mound. That gives the other team a huge advantage knowing the two of you aren't working together. You're both damn lucky we won this game tonight. Tomorrow afternoon better be a completely different atmosphere between the two of you. Am I clear?"

"Yes," they said together.

As soon as she dismissed them, both women bolted from the locker room. Graham was so ready to be out of there she nearly got a speeding ticket on her way home.

~

Graham ignored Dashtin's jabbing and went straight to the shower when she walked in. She stripped and stood under the hot water until the muscles in her body felt limp. She spread the soap around her body, shampooed her hair, and rinsed off. She was so tired and emotionally drained that she almost forgot to condition her hair before getting out. She put on a T-shirt and warm up pants and walked out to the living room.

"I ordered a pizza," Dashtin said as Graham sat down on the couch and put her feet up on the table.

"That's good. I'm starving," Graham said, stretching her tired, sore muscles. "What a day."

"The first baseman was cute," Dashtin said.

"Seriously? We have a horrible game and you're checking out the other team's players." Graham shook her head. "Maybe you should pay more attention to the game next time. I had my ass chewed twice!"

"How much trouble are you in?"

"She was pissed, but it wasn't too bad. Now, if it happens again tomorrow we're all toast," Graham said.

"What's Bailey's problem?"

"Dashtin, she's not the only problem. The entire team played like shit to start with."

"Yeah, well it doesn't help when your pitcher hands them bases and scoring runs."

"She's got a lot on her shoulders and your little dig probably didn't help matters much."

"Are you defending her?" Dashtin growled.

"Damn it, Dash. She's the pitcher. I'm the catcher. We have to be on the same page. You know that. All I'm saying is maybe you should apologize for calling her a kid."

"Fine," she said, picking up her cell phone. She texted a quick message to Bailey and tossed the phone back down. "Are you happy now?"

Graham sighed a frustrated breath. "Coach Parker and Coach Walker are riding my ass as it is. I don't need shit from you too."

~

Early the next afternoon, the Pioneers took to the field in their second of the three game series. Bailey came out pitching with precision, striking out every other batter with the exception of a stray ball or two caused by a wild pitch. Dashtin was all over the place catching pop-ups. Graham was managing the game flawlessly from home plate by stopping the base stealers, crowding the plate when runners tried to go home, and calling the right pitches.

The score was one to five in the fifth when Whitney stepped up to bat. She hit a ground ball that went between the second baseman and short stop allowing an RBI and setting her up in scoring position from second base with a double play. Vanessa went up behind her and was hit by a wild pitch that advanced her to first base. The other team made a quick pitching change and Dashtin batted next, hitting a fly ball way out in left field but it was caught giving her the second out.

Graham stepped up to the plate. She swung the bat a few times before taking her stance. The pitcher threw a strike on the first pitch and Graham sat back on it. The next pitch was inside and low for ball one. The third pitch was also low but further out. Graham shifted her weight to swing the bat low and up as hard as she could. A loud crack sounded as the bat connected with the ball, sending it all the way to the parking lot across the fence. Graham was already halfway to first before she realized she'd hit a home run with two RBIs. She jogged around the bases and was crowded to the ground by all of her teammates when she reached home plate. The score went to nine-one and because they were up by eight at the bottom of the fifth inning, the game was run-ruled over. The home team fans cheered loudly.

"Hell yeah, baby!" Dashtin yelled, picking Graham up and swinging her around.

Graham laughed and hugged her teammates and friends as they lined up to shake the hands of the players on the opposing team. This was only the fifth home run in her career at UCO.

The team was still cheering as they gathered their equipment and walked into the locker room.

"You really came together out there today, ladies. I'm proud of you. Way to show them whose house they were in! We still have one more game to prepare for against them tomorrow, but I'll let you go celebrate. This is what winning should feel like, remember that. Graham, I'm glad to see you and Bailey working together. You called a hell of a game from the plate and that last at bat was priceless," Coach Walker said. She high-fived each team member before leaving the locker room.

Helena walked up to Graham, placing her hand on her shoulder. "You had a great game today. Maybe you can show me how to bat like that sometime."

Graham nodded and politely smiled before walking away.

"She might as well put a sign on her forehead that says 'I wanna do the catcher,'" Dashtin exclaimed.

"Oh well, want to and going to are totally different things," Graham replied.

"Graham and Bailey, I'd like to talk to you before you leave," Coach Parker said.

"I'll see you at home," Dashtin said. "By the way, the team is going to *Sister Fred's* tonight so don't make any plans. You're coming with me, Captain."

Graham smiled and walked out of the locker room towards Coach Parker's office.

"You had a great game," Bailey said in the hallway.

"No, *we* had a great game. I may have hit a home run, but you struck out a lot of batters," Graham said as she held the door for Bailey to walk in ahead of her.

"You two are finally learning to communicate. I knew the combination would work out and you two ladies would be great together. There's still a lot of room for improvement and we'll work on that next week. Don't party too hard tonight. We still have another game tomorrow and we need to end this weekend on a winning streak."

"Do you need a ride?" Graham asked when they stepped back into the hallway.

"No, Alex is here. My dad finally got around to getting my car totaled by the dealer so the insurance check should hopefully arrive in the next few weeks so I should be getting a car before the semester ends, I hope. But knowing my dad he will wait until the summer so I can come home and pick it out."

"That's good."

"Are you going to *Sister Fred's*?" Bailey asked.

"The team usually goes there to celebrate great games so I'll be there."

"See you tonight then."

Chapter 7

Graham walked into *Sister Fred's* and maneuvered through the crowd near the bar and dance floor with Dashtin close to her back.

"I can't believe how packed it is this early," Dashtin said in her ear.

"It's because there's a band tonight," Graham said.

They quickly found the team gathered around a small group of tables pushed together and covered with appetizers. The upperclassmen had a couple pitchers of beer on their end of the table. That's where Graham and Dashtin sat.

"It's about time you got here," Whitney said, handing them glasses for the pitcher. "The band is awesome."

"You know we can't go anywhere in a hurry. Dashtin has to primp in front of the mirror for an hour." Graham poured herself and Dashtin a beer and cheered glasses with Whitney, who agreed with her statement.

Dashtin rolled her eyes. Taking a sip of the light beer, she scanned the dance floor. She raised an eyebrow when her eyes landed on an unexpected sight. She watched the two women dancing together. The song was fast, but it was fairly obvious they were together with the moves they were making. She tried to nudge Graham with her elbow, but she'd moved closer to Whitney to hear what she was saying over the loud music. Dashtin finally got her attention when the couple sat down at the other end of the table.

"What?" Graham said.

Dashtin nodded in the opposite direction. Graham looked past her in time to see Bailey getting very cozy with a brown-haired girl. She raised an eyebrow and looked at Dashtin.

"I told you she wasn't straight," Dashtin said.

"Who's that with Bailey?" Graham asked.

Whitney shrugged. "I think her name is Alex or something."

"That's Alex?" Graham nearly spit beer all over Whitney.

"What's wrong?"

"Nothing, I assumed Alex was her overprotective boyfriend not girlfriend."

Whitney laughed and shrugged. "There are more mailboxes in the world than you think."

"You and your secret words," Graham laughed. "So now we're calling lesbians, mailboxes?"

"Yes," Whitney said. "You can't very well shout 'hey look at that lesbian over there', but if you say 'look at that mailbox' it's more casual and less blunt."

"Alright, mailbox it is." Graham sipped her beer. "Did you hear this, Dashtin? We're now calling lesbians, mailboxes. It's the new code word, spread it around."

48

"Hey," Dashtin said. "Isn't that the team we beat today?"

All three women watched a bunch of girls putting tables together nearby.

"Looks like it," Whitney said.

"I wonder if any of them are mailboxes?" Graham said. Whitney cheered glasses with her as they laughed.

"Graham, guess who's here," Dashtin teased.

Graham didn't have to look too far. Her eyes landed on the Latina headed her way.

"Speaking of mailboxes," Graham said under her breath.

"Hey everyone," Helena said, staring at Graham. She sat down in the empty seat across from her.

"Coach," Whitney replied.

"Oh please, I'm just like all of you. Leave the coaching to Walker and Parker."

"Dance with me," Dashtin grabbed Graham's hand pulling her up out of her chair before she could respond.

They always had a good time flirting when they danced. It was innocent and a lot fun. The band played a few fast songs that kept them on the floor, spinning and twisting back and forth. Graham pulled Dashtin into her arms from behind, grinding against her backside. Dashtin spun in her arms, their lips inches apart. She smiled and laughed, pushing Graham away with her hand in the center of her chest.

They were so busy playing around on the dance floor that they missed a few of the other team members joining them. Graham and Dashtin sat down when the band started playing country music. Bailey and Alex passed them on their way to the dance floor. Graham couldn't keep her eyes off the small brunette, in her tight jeans, keeping perfect rhythm with the beat. She turned away when Alex pulled Bailey close, grinding against her petite, toned body.

Graham poured herself a second beer and drank a long sip.

"Aren't you passed your limit?" Whitney teased.

Graham flipped her the bird. "You know I can drink you all under the table. I just choose not to," she said as her eyes found the dance floor once again.

"Want to dance?" Helena said close to her ear.

Graham hadn't noticed that the Latina student coach moved to the chair next to her which had been previously occupied by Dashtin who was strangely missing from the group.

"No thanks," Graham said to her before turning back to Whitney. "Where's Dashtin?"

"No idea," Whitney said with a shrug.

Another fast song came on and Graham turned back to Helena. "Come on," she said as she stood up. Helena grinned from ear to ear.

Graham was careful not to touch Helena despite her advances. They danced together for the next couple of fast songs. As soon as a slow song started, they walked back towards the table. Bailey was standing by her chair when they walked by her.

"I thought you only dance with Dashtin," she said.

Graham spun around. She looked down at the young woman sitting next to Bailey's empty chair then back at Bailey's questioning green eyes.

"I guess there's a lot we don't know about each other," she said and walked away in time to see Dashtin coming from the bathroom.

"Are you ready to go?" Dashtin asked, reaching for her beer.

"Dash, what have you done now?" Graham sighed.

Dashtin grinned, wiggling her eyebrows.

"You didn't."

"Oh I did. Twice actually," Dashtin laughed.

Graham shook her head. "Is she even gay?"

"Who knows?"

"Where've you been?" Whitney asked Dashtin. "You missed Graham dancing with Helena."

"You danced with her?" Dashtin raised an eyebrow.

"You just screwed a girl from the other team in the bathroom!"

"No! You didn't?" Whitney laughed.

Graham cocked her head to the side and waited for Dashtin to speak.

"Oh my god, you did! Who was it?" Whitney squealed.

"The first baseman, I'm guessing. This should make the game all that more interesting tomorrow," Graham added.

"She followed me in there. What was I supposed to do, say no?"

"I can't say anything. I slept with you too, but that was way back in my sophomore year when I was stupid and didn't know better," Whitney exclaimed.

"I think I've had about enough excitement for one night. Are you riding with me?" Graham asked. She loved her best friend, but there was no way she'd ever sleep with her. That's what made them so close.

"Yes," Dashtin said, jumping up to follow her outside.

Chapter 8

The third game of the weekend series started off great for the Pioneers because the opposing teams' first baseman was playing with a bundle of nerves, dropping balls and making horrible throws. The other team was helping them stay ahead in the game with seven runs scored in four innings, but Bailey's off pitching in the fifth inning allowed them to start making a comeback, bringing the score to four-seven.

"What did you do to that girl?" Whitney teased.

"The same thing I did to you," Dashtin countered with a grin.

Whitney rolled her eyes, shaking her head.

Graham walked back into the dugout after hitting a fly ball for an out. "What did I miss?" she said as she began putting her catching gear back on.

"Nothing interesting," Whitney said as they watched Vanessa strike out and Claudia hit a foul ball for the third out.

The first batter of the sixth inning was a slap-hitter. Bailey threw a screwball that turned in and the batter stepped too far inside and the ball hit her in the left forearm. The next batter was the first baseman. She struck out in three straight pitches. On the last pitch Graham threw the ball out to Dashtin to get her attention. She shrugged and threw it to Bailey.

The next two batters managed to hit ground balls, advancing the first batter and filling the bases. Graham gave Bailey the signal for a screwball and she shook her head no. She gave her the signal again and Bailey visibly shook her head no. Graham gave in and called for a rise ball which Bailey threw out of the strike zone causing ball-one. When she threw a second pitch into the dirt Graham pulled up her mask and ran out to the mound.

"What's going on?" she asked.

"I hit that girl."

"Bailey, batters are going to get hit. It happens. Besides she was a crazy slap hitter that stepped into the damn ball. Take a deep breath and throw the ball the way you and I both know you can throw it. You've got this." Graham said with a grin before running back to the plate.

Bailey threw a curve and then another rise ball for two strikes. With a two and two count she threw a screwball on the outside of the strike zone and the batter chased it for the third strike and third out of the inning. Graham breathed a sigh of relief as she raced into the dugout.

"Good job," Graham wrapped her arm around Bailey's shoulders. Bailey moved into her and Graham stiffened. She casually moved away and sat down on the bench next to Dashtin.

"That was a close one."

"She lets the freshman nerves get to her."

"You sure do defend her a lot," Dashtin said.

"Why do you have such a problem with her?"

"She always looks at me like she hates me. I think she's got it bad for you."

"Oh please. Are we really going to go down that road again? She has a girlfriend and I'm not interested."

"Oh sure. I've seen the way you look at her and that whole girlfriend thing is a joke. She only brought that girl around to see what your reaction would be."

"I won't deny looking at her. She's beautiful, but she's a freshman and I'm not going there. That's your thing, not mine."

"Fine. You might want to let her know that though."

Graham turned her head in time to see Bailey looking her way. She nodded and turned back to Dashtin who had an 'I told you so' look on her face. She stood up and walked to the fence where the rest of the team was standing watching the game.

The seventh inning came up and Bailey threw every pitch perfectly, ending the inning and the game on three batters. The team hugged her, patted her back, and slapped her butt as they celebrated another win and shutout. They quickly slapped hands with the other team and collected their gear.

"Way to go," Graham squeezed Bailey's shoulder as she walked past her towards the locker room.

"Great come back, ladies. Bailey, you and Graham need to work on ball control this week. The rest of you be ready to work this week. We have practice Tuesday, Wednesday, and Thursday. We're away at Washington next weekend, as you all know. The bus leaves at nine a.m. Friday so make sure you're not late," Coach Walker said, looking directly at Dashtin. "Now, go celebrate. I'll see you Tuesday."

When the coaching staff left the room, Whitney called out, "Hey Dash, there's someone waiting outside for you."

The blood drained from Dashtin's face. Graham laughed and ducked as Dashtin tossed her glove at her head. She sighed and walked towards the door.

Whitney hid behind Graham as Dashtin opened the door and looked around. No one was there.

"You ass," she yelled.

"We all owe you this win. Everyone say thanks to Dashtin for taking one for the team and banging the other team's first baseman," Whitney squealed as Dashtin grabbed her and put her in a headlock, rubbing her knuckles on the top of her head. Most of the team knew what had happened anyway so they were all laughing. Graham noticed Bailey off to the side, sitting in front of her locker with her back to the room.

"No wonder she couldn't handle the ball. I thought maybe she was sick or hurt or something," one of their teammates said.

"Yeah or something," Graham said with a grin.

"We won the game didn't we?" Dashtin shook her head laughing.

"Hey Dash, maybe you can help us out with Washington too," Whitney teased.

"I'm going on strike!" Dashtin tossed her glove in her locker and slammed the door. She was still smiling and shaking her head.

"Yeah right," Graham said. "I'll believe that when I see it."

"Me too," Whitney and Vanessa said together.

'I'm out of here, ladies. See you all this week," Graham said. "Dash, I'm stopping for take-out on my way home so you're on your own for dinner."

"That's fine. I'll grab something."

~

Graham was about to unlock her Jeep but turned around when she heard her name.

"I wanted to thank you for what you said out there today," Bailey said. "I haven't hit anyone since my sophomore year of high school. I hit a girl in the head and gave her a concussion. I stopped pitching for a few months after that."

"Wow. Today was nothing like that, Bailey. It was mostly the batter's own fault for stepping into the box."

"I know that now, but..."

"Look at me. You didn't hurt anyone today and you picked yourself right back up. You're a great pitcher. Mistakes are going to happen."

Bailey sighed. "I know. Anyway, I just wanted to say thanks," she said turning to walk away.

"Hey, if you don't have any plans with Alex, I'm going to grab something to eat. Nothing fancy, probably just drive-thru."

"Do you see Alex here?" Bailey said.

"I'd never seen her before the other night so I have no idea."

"She's working tonight," Bailey said, walking around to the passenger side.

"What do you want to eat?"

"Whatever is fine with me."

Graham rode through the first drive-thru she saw. They both ordered burgers and fries and she pulled out of the parking lot, going in the opposite direction of the school. Graham drove across town and pulled into a small parking lot.

"Have you ever been here?" she asked, cutting the engine.

"No."

Graham got out and waited for Bailey to join her. "This is Harmon Park. It's sort of my thinking spot. I come out here sometimes and sit on the bench watching the river flow by," she said, walking towards the bench down by the water. There were a few street lights in the parking lot, but the water was lit by the moonlight.

"I can see why you come here," Bailey said, taking a seat next to her.

"In the summer there are ducks everywhere looking for food." Graham sat next to her and opened the bag of food. "We're safe this time of year. It's too cold for the ducks."

"It is pretty cold," Bailey said.

"I have a jacket in the Jeep."

"I'm okay, thanks." Bailey smiled.

"Are you excited about our first away game?"

"More nervous than anything probably, but yeah it's exciting."

"You'll get over what happened today and move on to a new team and a new group of batters. Washington is our first conference game and they're usually a pretty good team. We just need to stay focused and we'll have a good weekend," Graham said.

"I hope so. You make it sound so easy." Bailey finished eating and put her trash in the bin next to the bench. She sat much closer to Graham when she sat back down. Graham noticed she was shaking slightly.

"You're cold," she said.

"I'll be fine," Bailey said. "It's beautiful here. I'm going to have to remember to come back during the day and especially in the summer."

"It's a great place to sit and think or write a paper." Graham smiled.

"I hope you don't mind me borrowing your thinking spot. I use to go to the old pond at the edge of my family's farm and watch the ducks swim for hours. It was sort of a place to go and disappear from the world for a little while," Bailey said.

"Do you miss home?"

"I did at first. It's not easy being so far away, but after I went home for the holidays I was ready to leave again."

"You still have a while before you graduate. Do you think you will go back to Texas afterwards?"

"I honestly don't know. Being a business major gives me a lot of opportunities so I guess I will see where that takes me. My family has had a dairy farm for three generations and my dad added quarter horse and pony breeding when he took it over. As a kid I often dreamed of owning the farm one day. I'm the first one in my family to go to college, so I will probably end up as a farmer with a business degree down the road," Bailey said, smiling.

"You could turn it into a dude ranch," Graham teased.

"My great-grandfather would roll over in his grave!" Bailey laughed.

Graham looked at Bailey's eyes sparkling in the moonlight. The sound of her laughter made Graham's chest ache. She didn't think she'd ever wanted anything more in her life, but she knew better than to get involved with the enigmatic freshman.

"What's wrong? You look deep in thought."

"I'm fine. We should probably go," Graham said.

Bailey stood and grabbed Graham's hand when she started to walk away.

"Thanks for bringing me here, Graham."

Graham squeezed the small, cold hand holding hers. "You're welcome," she replied softly.

Bailey held her hand as they walked back to the parking lot. Graham unlocked her door and held it open for her. Bailey brushed against her as she moved to climb in the Jeep. They rode in silence as Graham drove across town. When they arrived at the dorm Bailey grabbed Graham's hand, running her thumb over the top of it casually.

"Have a good night," Graham said, squeezing the hand holding hers.

Chapter 9

The week went by quickly due to grueling practices. By Friday Graham was ready for the weekend to be over. She and Dashtin arrived on time for the bus. They went to work helping the rest of the team load the bus with the equipment and suitcases.

"It's time to load up, ladies. We need to get on the road. Pick a seat buddy and get on the bus," Coach Walker said.

Dashtin grabbed Graham's hand and pulled her along. They sat behind Whitney and Vanessa at the back of the bus. Bailey and Claudia wound up sitting on the aisle across from them.

"I know you brought food," Whitney said when she peered over the top of her seat an hour into the trip. "Where is it?"

Dashtin shrugged. "I must have forgot, damn."

Graham laughed as Dashtin opened a package of M&M's and gave her a handful.

Whitney's head popped back up in time to snatch the package. She and Vanessa shared the rest of them. Dashtin pulled another bag out of her pocket and smiled at Graham who was watching a movie on her phone.

"How many hours do we have left?" Dashtin joked.

"Five, now shut up or go sit somewhere else," Graham chided. She was watching a movie about a handful of scientists trying to find a cure to a disease that was secretly killing people all over the world.

"Well, excuse me." Dashtin got up and moved a few rows up to sit with some other teammates. They were playing a game on their phones with Vanessa and Whitney.

"What are you watching?" Bailey leaned over and asked Graham.

Graham pulled her headphones from her ear. "A movie about biological warfare."

Bailey got up and sat down in Dashtin's vacant seat. She held her hand out for one of the ear phones and Graham gave it to her. Graham moved her phone sitting on the tray table in front of her, so Bailey could see the movie too.

Three hours later, Dashtin was surprised when she walked back to her seat. Bailey was in her seat asleep with her head on Graham's shoulder. Graham was asleep with her head against Bailey's.

"What the hell?" she said.

"They passed out a while ago. Must've been a shitty movie," Whitney said. "Aren't they cute?"

"No, they're not," she growled.

"Jealous?" Whitney teased.

"No, I'm not jealous. Bailey has a girlfriend and she's still trying to get in Graham's pants. Graham's too good to get hurt by her and I'm not going to let it happen."

"Oh Dash, leave them alone. Graham's not going to hook-up with a freshman anyway. She's smarter than that. I have noticed Helena making goo-goo eyes at her though," Whitney said.

"Yeah, Graham's turned her down half a dozen times but she keeps coming back," Dashtin said.

"That's a little creepy," Vanessa said.

"I think it's funny."

"You would," Whitney said. "Go get in your seat and take a nap. We still have an hour and a half."

"Half-pint's in my seat passed out on my best friend in case you forgot."

"Go sit with Helena," Whitney laughed.

Dashtin rolled her eyes and walked back to the seat she had been using earlier, in the middle of the bus.

Graham awoke when the bus came to a stop at the hotel. The warm body next to her stirred and she looked at the dark head of hair on her shoulder. Bailey sat up and stretched as she turned her head in Graham's direction.

"I guess I missed the end of the movie," she said shyly.

"Yeah, me too," Graham replied.

Bailey handed the earphone she'd been wearing to Graham and moved back to her seat to gather her things.

"It's about time you woke up, sleeping beauty," Dashtin said to Graham.

"I didn't even know I fell asleep. Why didn't you wake me?"

"I wanted to but you and Bailey were so cute all cuddled together," she said sarcastically.

Graham laughed. "Oh, she's just a kid. I think you're mad it wasn't you all cuddled with me," she teased.

"You're damn right. I had to listen to Katie snore most of the way!"

"I didn't tell you to get up, did I? That was your own fault. Now, come on, I'm ready to get off this damn bus," Graham said.

~

After everyone got settled into their rooms, the team ate dinner at the hotel restaurant and loaded the bus once again to head over to the field for their early evening game. Dashtin sat next to Graham in their original bus seats.

"I still don't understand why Coach Parker is making you room with Bailey. She's should be with Claudia. They're both freshmen," Dashtin said.

"I wasn't expecting it and don't exactly care for the arrangement either, but I'm not going to argue," Graham said. "It's better than rooming with Helena."

"I'd room with her."

"You'd room with anyone with tits and ass," Graham said.

"Ha-ha."

"Who are you rooming with?" Graham asked.

"Whitney. Apparently, she and Vanessa got split up too. Vanessa is with Claudia for some kind of mentoring thing or something. I think the coaches have lost their minds."

"Well, at least I know she won't sleep with you. She said once was enough."

Dashtin laughed. "Don't worry, I'm not interested anyway."

Graham shook her head and put her headphones on. She liked to listen to music on her playlist before their games. Dashtin watched her as she bobbed her head to the beat and took one of her ear phones out and put it in her own ear. They were both head bobbing and singing along by the time the bus pulled into the parking lot at the ball field.

~

The game started slowly for the Pioneers. Most of the team was tired and had bus lag from the six hour drive. In the bottom of the third they were down one to zero. Graham squatted at the plate and gave the signal for a rise ball. Bailey flinched when the ball came off her hand. She knew it was going to be bad. The ball began rising too early and by the time it crossed the plate Graham had to stand up and jump to catch it, causing her to fall backwards hard, knocking the wind out of her. When she didn't immediately get up the umpire stopped the game and Coach Walker and Helena ran to her.

"I'm okay," Graham said, sitting up.

"Take it easy," Helena said. She was bent down next to Graham with her hand on her back.

"You knocked the wind out yourself. Take a few deep breaths," Coach Walker said from her other side.

Dashtin and Bailey both ran in to check on their catcher and team captain.

"She's fine. She lost her breath when she fell," Coach Walker said.

"Yeah, no thanks to you," Dashtin said to Bailey.

"The ball slipped," Bailey said. "It was an accident."

"Every other pitch from you is an 'accident'."

"Alright, both of you go back to your positions and stay there!" Coach Walker yelled.

Graham stood up on her own and stretched her back out. "I'm good, coach."

Coach Walker patted her shoulder and went back to the dugout with Helena.

They'd managed to get out of the inning, but not before the other team scored again after another wild pitch that Graham had to dive for. It advanced the base runner from first to third. The next batter brought her home with an RBI.

The next two innings had gone the same way with wild pitches at the plate and infielders missing ground balls. The Pioneers were down three to zero going into the seventh. Whitney struck out and Vanessa hit a double. Graham hit a ground ball that the shortstop missed, allowing her to take first base and advancing Vanessa to third. Claudia came up to the plate with the potential tying run. She hit a pop-up that nearly cleared the fence. The centerfielder dove and missed the ball. Vanessa ran home, Graham crossed the plate behind her, and Claudia was stopped at third. The next batter struck out easily.

Down by one with two outs, Katie the sophomore outfielder stepped up to the plate. She wasn't the strongest hitter on the team, but her ground balls were fierce. The other team called for a pitcher change which turned out to be a huge mistake. The very first pitch the new pitcher threw went right down the middle instead of curving. Katie swung the bat, connecting with the ball and pushing it all the way to the left field fence. Since she wasn't a huge hitter everyone on the other team was playing inside. No one anticipated the fly ball.

By the time one of the outfielders finally reached the ball and fielded it, Claudia had crossed home plate and Katie was running for home. The other team's catcher jumped in front of Katie with the ball coming to her in the air. Katie dove to the ground, sliding around the catcher. Her hand grazed the plate just as the catcher was catching the ball with no time to reach down and tag her.

The entire Pioneer team ran from the dugout, shouting and cheering. The coaches pulled the team back together. The inning wasn't over. Bailey batted next. She wasn't the best batter, but she was a fast base runner. The first pitch to her was a strike followed by another strike. On the third pitch Bailey got nervous and swung. She hit a pop-up that the second base player easily caught for the third out.

The Pioneers took the field for the last time. Bailey struck out the first batter and walked the second with crazy pitches. The third batter came up and hit a ground ball over the third baseman's head, allowing two runners on base. The next batter hit a foul ball down the line and the third baseman dove to catch it. They had one out to go and the miserable game would be over.

Graham called for a drop ball and regretted it as soon as it left Bailey's hand. The ball was coming in too low. The slap-hitter smacked the low ball down into the dirt causing Graham to have to scramble for it. She was able to throw it to first, but not before the runner cleared the bag. Graham shook her head and squatted back down behind the plate.

The next batter swung at a screw ball for a strike before hitting three fouls in a row. Bailey's nerves took over with the count zero to two, causing her to throw two balls out of the strike zone and bumping the count to two and two. Bailey setup and released her next pitch. The ball looked like it was going to cross the center of the plate before curving wickedly to the left. The batter swung and the ball went right around the top of the bat as it curved. Graham jumped into the air and the rest of the team quickly met her at the plate, cheering and jumping up and down. They'd won the game by the skin of their teeth and were thankful that the game was finally over.

Chapter 10

Once the post game celebration and courtesy hand slapping with the other team was over, they began loading their equipment on the bus.

"What a mess," Whitney said.

"Yeah, no kidding. At least we won," Dashtin said as they boarded the bus.

"Don't get comfortable, ladies." Coach Walker was standing in the middle of the aisle as the bus began to pull away. "That was by far the worst game I've ever seen. I honestly have no idea how we won and that's not a win in my book. I don't know if you were all tired or ate too much dinner or just plain didn't give a shit whether we won or lost! Every single player on this team played sloppy. Bailey, you can't throw the ball all over the place and expect Graham to catch it every time. You have to work on ball control. Whitney and Dashtin, your uniforms are way too clean. It's no wonder with all of the groundballs that you neglected to dive for. I could go on and on all night. We looked like a monkey screwing a football out there and it will not happen again."

The bus pulled into the hotel parking lot and rolled to a stop. No one budged. All eyes were on Coach Walker.

"You all need to think long and hard about the way you've been playing and make a decision. Do you want to be on this team or not? If you do then you need to take that field every game with everything you've got, including Pioneer pride! Now, go get some sleep. We have a team meeting in the conference room after breakfast and then we're going over to a local high school for practice," she said before walking off the bus.

"Man she's pissed," Dashtin said.

"No kidding," Whitney replied.

"Do you blame her? We all played like shit. I don't know how we keep winning these games," Graham added.

"It didn't help that you knocked yourself out chasing down *another* crazy pitch," Dashtin said loud enough for Bailey to hear. "You have every right to be pissed too."

"I am pissed! Do you think I like jumping and diving like an idiot for ball after ball? My entire body hurts! But, the whole team is to blame for the way we played today," Graham said.

Whitney and Graham walked into the elevator followed by Vanessa. The door closed before Bailey could catch it and none of them bothered to hold it for her.

"I want my own room," Graham said when the doors opened again at their floor.

Whitney laughed. "Me too, but hey we can't have everything we want," she said, bumping shoulders with Dashtin. "At least you don't snore."

"Should I be worried about you two sharing a room?" Graham raised an eyebrow.

"Room is the keyword, Graham. Room, not bed, and trust me that's all we're sharing," Whitney said, stopping at the door to their room. "Get some sleep. Tomorrow is probably going to be hell."

"Should I be worried about you?" Dashtin asked when Graham walked past her.

"Oh please, that's the last thing in the world that will ever happen. I guarantee it," Graham said, walking to her room on the opposite side of the hall and a few doors down.

~

"Thanks for holding the elevator," Bailey said through gritted teeth when she walked into the room.

Graham was on the other side of the two double beds sitting in a chair, staring out of the window. She was still in her uniform minus her cleats and socks with her jersey pulled loose from her pants. The first few buttons were undone revealing the top of her chest and part of her black sports bra.

"It was an accident," Graham said, sarcastically using the same term that Bailey had used on the field. She stood up and walked close enough to touch Bailey as she passed by her on her way to the shower.

Graham stood under the hot water, willing her tense muscles to relax. She shampooed her hair and lathered

71

her body with soap before quickly rinsing the dirt and grime of the horrible game down the drain. She put on a robe and towel-dried her short hair before finally dressing in a T-shirt and shorts. Graham noticed Bailey sitting in the same chair by the window when she opened the bathroom door.

Bailey stood up and walked past her to the bathroom without saying a word. Graham turned the TV on and tossed the comforter from her bed to the floor before sitting on the bed. Her freshman year she'd taken samples from every hotel she had stayed in during the softball season and tested them all in a lab for her final exam project. The amount of biological matter detected had disgusted her and she swore she'd never use a hotel comforter again.

She was flipping channels on the TV when she heard the shower stop. Seconds later, the blow dryer started and ran for a few minutes before it stopped. Bailey emerged freshly scrubbed wearing a thin T-shirt and the smallest pair of shorts Graham had ever seen. She brushed her hair over her shoulder where it fell in loose waves. She raised an eyebrow and looked at Graham when she noticed the comforter on the floor.

Graham turned her head back to the TV and continued to channel surf.

"Are you going to ignore me all night?" Bailey huffed.

"There's nothing to say."

"I have plenty to say," Bailey growled. "First of all, I'm not the only one to blame. I seem to recall you missing a few balls all on your own that were in the zone.

Second, I've about had it with your girlfriend getting in my face. She needs to mind her own business."

Graham stood up and threw the remote on her bed. She was tired and frustrated and Bailey's anger only fueled the fire burning deep inside her.

"You're damn right I missed a few catches." Graham yelled, walking closer to her. "You try catching balls flying in all directions especially after being dropped on your ass so hard you can't breathe. Don't even start on me when that is all your fault."

"I said I didn't mean to throw that ball the way I did. It came off my hand wrong. I don't need it thrown back in my face over and over. Do you even realize how it made me feel when I saw you lying on the ground not moving? It scared me to death, Graham. So, don't go acting like it was nothing to me. I'm trying to carry this damn team on my back and that's difficult enough for anyone to do, let alone a freshman. I'm sorry I let the nerves get to me," Bailey growled, stepping close enough to smell the soap Graham had washed with. "I don't need the entire team riding my ass. The coaches are doing a great job on their own."

"Then you need to trust me when I call pitches and trust the rest of your team to field the ball if it gets hit. Most of all, you need to stop calling Dashtin my girlfriend. That's starting to really piss me off. She's my best friend and has every right to say something when I get hurt. Besides, you're the one with a girlfriend all over you, not me." Graham snarled.

"That's where you're wrong. Not that it's any of your business but Alex and I aren't together. She wants me."

"What do you want?"

"You, Graham. I want you," Bailey said.

Graham bent her head, slowly pressing her lips to Bailey's. She ran her tongue around the edge of her mouth. As the kiss deepened, she put her hands on Bailey's waist and pushed her back against the wall. Holding her there with her body tightly against Bailey's, she grabbed her hands, placing them just above her head on the wall.

She sucked Bailey's tongue between her lips and Bailey's hips moved against her in response. Graham let go of Bailey's hands and pushed the thin T-shirt up, revealing Bailey's naturally tan, lithe body and perky round breasts with dark nipples. She moved her mouth to Bailey's neck, running her lips from her collar to her ear as her hands slid over silky smooth skin and up to caress her breasts.

Bailey moaned when Graham lowered her head to her breasts, licking and sucking back and forth. She tangled her hands in Graham's short hair, pulling her up for another searing kiss. Graham pulled back long enough to remove Bailey's wadded up T-shirt, tossing it behind her onto the floor before kissing her again breathlessly. Her leg slipped between Bailey's thighs. She felt the wetness coat her leg as Bailey moved against her, riding up and down.

Graham reached down with both hands cupping Bailey's firm butt, picking her up. Bailey wrapped her legs around Graham's waist as she carried her over to her bed. Graham laid Bailey on her back and pulled her own shirt off before crawling on top of her. Their skin burned as their breasts and stomachs molded together when she slid up Bailey's body.

Bailey locked her legs around Graham and rolled her over so that she was on top. She sat up, straddling Graham's hips and grabbed her hands placing them on her breasts. Graham squeezed softly, flicking the hard nipples with her thumbs before moving her hands lower. Bailey's skin was so warm and silky smooth, like nothing she'd ever felt before.

Bailey brought one of Graham's hands to her mouth, slowly running her tongue over each finger before biting her thumb and sucking the tip. Graham's hips moved involuntarily against Bailey. She grinned and repeated the gesture with Graham's other hand before lying back down on top of her. Graham ran her hands over Bailey's bare back, over the shorts that covered her tight little ass, to the top of her thighs. She was surprised when she moved her hands under the shorts to squeeze Bailey's cheeks and discovered there was nothing under the shorts.

"Touch me," Bailey whispered.

She reached between Bailey's legs coating her fingers with wetness. Bailey kissed Graham's lips while moving herself back and forth over the fingers touching her.

Graham suddenly rolled Bailey onto her back and peeled the wet shorts off of her, tossing them on the floor. She wiggled out of her own shorts, tossing them in the same direction. She pushed Bailey's thighs apart and bent her head, tasting the glistening folds as she licked up and down softly applying more and more pressure with each pass of her tongue. Graham felt a tug on her hair from Bailey's hand as Bailey's hips rose to meet her stroke for stroke.

Graham kept her eyes on Bailey, watching her moan and writhe under her touch. Bailey ran her free hand over her own chest squeezing her breasts one at a time back and forth. Graham pulled her mouth away causing Bailey to gasp. She smiled and slid her body along Bailey's, placing wet kisses over her stomach and breasts before reaching her mouth. Bailey licked Graham's lips, loving the way she tasted on her.

Graham moved her hand down between Bailey's legs, sliding through the wetness. She slipped two fingers easily inside of her. Bailey groaned, opening her legs wider so Graham could go deeper. Her hips moved to meet each thrust of Graham's fingers as Graham kissed her hard, sucking and biting her bottom lip.

"Oh god, you feel so good...," Bailey panted, wrapping her arms and legs around Graham. She ran her short nails down Graham's back, rocking her body back and forth under her as Graham pushed her fingers harder and deeper into her.

Bailey stopped moving and pushed Graham onto her back, careful not to let the fingers slip out of her as she straddled Graham once again. Graham sat up, wrapping one arm around Bailey's waist as Bailey moved back and forth on the fingers buried deep inside her. Graham kissed her mouth and traced her tongue over her neck to the soft spot behind her ear and back again.

Bailey rode harder and harder until she groaned wildly like an animal. Pulling Graham's fingers out of her, she pushed her back and rubbed herself on Graham's stomach, coating her with hot wetness.

When her body began to relax, she adjusted her position and lay on Graham, kissing her tenderly before sliding down between her legs to take her into her mouth, licking and sucking. Graham's hips rose to meet her. She was taken off guard and it felt so good. She placed her hand on the back of Bailey's head, holding her mouth where she wanted. She was so close she nearly came just from touching Bailey.

Bailey pulled away teasingly as Graham's hips started to buck under her. Graham gasped, moving her hips up, trying to reach the mouth she so desperately wanted on her, but Bailey shook her head no. Instead, she pushed two fingers deep inside Graham causing her to moan loudly. Then, she pulled them all the way out only to start all over again. After the third time, she bent her head, licking and sucking Graham as she settle into a deep stroking rhythm that matched her fingers to her mouth.

"You're going to kill me," Graham wheezed, grasping at the bed sheets with one hand while holding Bailey's head with the other. Her entire body was writhing under Bailey.

Bailey grinned with her mouth still on Graham and her fingers buried inside of her, pushing deeper with each thrust of her hips. She pulled her mouth away and slid up Graham's body when she felt her tighten against her fingers. Their mouths connected for a searing kiss. Tasting herself on Bailey's tongue was enough to push Graham over the edge. She cried out, rocking her hips wildly against Bailey's hand until there was nothing left.

Graham was breathless. Her body felt like a limp noodle soaring through the sky. Reality began to sink in as Bailey's warm body curled up against her side. Graham rolled onto her side, wrapping her arms around

Bailey and kissing her tenderly. She wasn't exactly sure what this meant but it was too good not to see where it would go, at least for now anyway.

"I guess you did have a lot to say," Graham teased.

Bailey smiled. "Who said I was done talking?" she said pushing Graham onto her back.

Chapter 11

The next morning, Graham was sitting at breakfast scrolling the news on her phone when Dashtin sat down at her table.

"Good morning," Graham said.

Dashtin raised an eyebrow. "What's up?"

"What do you mean?"

"Good morning? Really? I've lived with you going on four years and I don't think you've ever said 'good morning' once."

"Well, we usually don't see each other for breakfast because unlike you I schedule my classes early. I'm usually gone before you even get up." Graham took a bite of her toast. "Besides, after yesterday I'm trying to have a fresh start for today."

"Uh huh," Dashtin said, snatching the last piece of toast from her plate.

"The blueberry pancakes are pretty good," Graham said.

"Pancakes, fruit, toast," Dashtin said, peered into the cup on the table. "And coffee? Did you skip dinner last night?"

"No. You sat right next to me. We did eat before the game though and I was starving afterwards but too pissed off to eat. I guess it caught up to me this morning."

Bailey walked into the dining area with Claudia and sat at Katie and Vanessa's table. Graham thought back to her conversation that morning with Bailey asking her not to say anything about their night together despite Bailey wanting to rub it in Dashtin's face.

"How did you sleep?" Dashtin asked.

"Actually, pretty good. Apparently, Bailey doesn't snore. How was your night?"

"Boring. Whitney wouldn't shut up about the game until almost midnight. I forgot how much she talks. If I remember correctly she even talks during sex," Dashtin said, reaching for Graham's coffee.

"You know better than to drink that," Graham said but it was too late. Dashtin took a long sip and practically spit it all over the table causing most of the people in the room to look their way.

"Yuck!" she spat.

"You know I like sugar in my coffee, you dipshit. Go get your own cup," Graham chided.

"That's disgusting. I don't know how you drink it with all of that sugar." Dashtin got up and walked over to the breakfast bar. She returned with a fresh cup of sugar-free coffee and a small plate of pancakes.

"So how do you remember Whitney talks during sex if you only slept with her once almost four years ago?" Graham asked.

"Because none of you will let me forget it," Dashtin said with her mouth full of pancakes.

"Let you forget what?" Whitney said, sitting in the empty chair at their table. She had a plate of fruit with a bagel.

"Nothing," Dashtin mumbled.

"How was your night?" Graham asked.

"Fine. Dash was the perfect gentleman or gentlewoman. I'm not sure exactly how that goes," Whitney said.

Dashtin rolled her eyes and Graham laughed.

"Good morning, ladies. I hope everyone slept well and ate a good breakfast. The bus leaves in twenty minutes for our practice session," Coach Walker announced.

"I'm not looking forward to this," Dashtin said.

"Who is?" Graham asked, getting up from the table.

~

Practice was grueling. Coach Walker and Helena hit pop-ups and ground balls for the team to practice catching and fielding while Coach Parker had Bailey pitching and Graham catching. After a half hour, Coach Parker sat Bailey and had the back-up pitcher, a junior named Sarah Wheat, warm-up and practice. She was a good pitcher and worked well in the second spot with two other pitchers behind her. Coach Parker had yet to pull Bailey from a game or even sit her out in a game and so far the strategy was working for her. Bailey was used to the back to back games since she'd been the only pitcher on her high school team.

"Let's wrap it up, ladies. We need to save our energy for the game this afternoon," Coach Walker said.

Everyone gathered their gear and headed for the bus. Graham shoved her catching gear into the compartment on the bottom of the bus and boarded along with the rest of her teammates. Whitney noticed her yawning as she walked down the aisle.

"I thought you said you slept well?" Whitney said as Graham sat down next to her.

"I did. I'm just worn out and I have a lot on my mind with my senior thesis," Graham said.

Dashtin pulled a bag of M&M's from the pocket of the seat in front of her. She offered some to Graham.

"I swear you hide things like a dog," Graham said.

Dashtin laughed. "I don't see you complaining as you share my snack."

"Nope, not at all," Graham said, reaching for another handful of candy pieces.

~

When the bus arrived back at the hotel Whitney announced her and Dashtin's room as the hangout for the next few hours until they had lunch and then left for their afternoon game. They had a couple of sets of cards and were planning to watch a movie.

"I might see you guys in a little bit," Graham said in the elevator. "I'm going to take a nap and then do some research."

"There's a nerd in every group," Whitney said.

Graham grinned sarcastically and walked to her room when the doors opened for their floor. She quickly stripped and stepped into the shower. The hot water soothed her aching muscles. It had been a while since she'd spent the night with a woman and her body was sore in places she forgot she had. She wasn't a one-night-stand kind of person and rarely dated since she broke things off with her cheating ex-girlfriend in the summer before her junior year.

She finished washing her hair and had just covered herself with soap when the shower curtain moved. Graham watched Bailey's naked body as she stepped inside, pulling the curtain closed.

"Shouldn't you be with the rest of the group?" Graham said, rinsing the soap from her body.

Bailey moved closer, running her hand up Graham's torso, stopping between her breasts. "I don't play poker and I've seen A League of Their Own a thousand and one times. I actually went to Claudia's room. She was showing me pictures on her computer of her nephew that was born yesterday. She's so mad she couldn't be there. She'd planned on going home next week for a few days but her sister went into labor early. Besides, I have better things to do," she said, running her hand back down Graham's body.

Graham stopped the wandering hand just before it grazed her between the legs. "You're playing with fire," she said.

"Good, I like it hot," Bailey teased.

Graham grabbed her other hand. Pushing both hands behind Bailey's back, she stepped up against her. "You might get burned," Graham said, bending and kissing her hard. She turned Bailey into the hot water and released her.

"Where are you going?" Bailey whimpered.

Graham smiled. "I'm squeaky clean. It's all yours." she said, stepping out of the shower leaving Bailey stunned.

A few minutes later Bailey finished showering and walked into the room to find Graham asleep on her bed. She dropped her towel and climbed on top of her.

"You're all wet!" Graham shrieked, squirming under the wet body covering hers.

"In more ways than one," Bailey said, biting her lower lip teasingly before kissing her and pulling back. "I can't believe you left me in the shower."

"You were in need of a shower," Graham replied, pushing Bailey up as she wriggled down the bed under her.

"Oh really?"

"I think you're in need of something else now." Graham grinned, pushing Bailey's hips over mouth, licking her softly.

"God yes," Bailey hissed, biting her bottom lip as she settled lower, opening herself further. She grabbed the headboard for support as she moved her hips back and forth over Graham's mouth, meeting her tongue stroke for stroke.

Graham licked long strokes then short circles, sucking Bailey into her mouth over and over while her hands roamed Bailey's lithe body from her thighs to her breasts. Bailey moaned and bit her own knuckles to keep from screaming as the waves of pleasure washed over her. She rode Graham's mouth until she could no longer hold on. Her muscles felt like jelly as she backed away, collapsing next to Graham.

Graham leaned over, kissing her deeply. A loud knock on the door scared them both back to reality. Bailey stumbled towards the bathroom on shaky legs while Graham dove for the sink to rinse her face and mouth.

Whoever was at the door knocked again and Graham walked over to the door pulling it open.

"It's about time," Dashtin and Whitney said.

"I was asleep and I think Bailey's in the shower," Graham said.

"We go to dinner in half an hour," Dashtin said.

"Is the party over already?" Bailey asked, emerging from the shower in a team T-shirt and warm-up pants. Her hair was much curlier than normal because she didn't blow dry it in her haste to jump in bed with Graham so it started to air dry.

"I was beginning to think the party was in here," Whitney said.

"Nope, no party. Just me and sleepy head over there," Bailey said. "Did I hear you say lunch is soon?"

"Yeah," Dashtin looked around the room. Bailey's bed was completely made and Graham's was a mess with the comforter and one of the pillows on the floor.

"Great, I'm starving," Bailey said, putting her socks and sneakers on. "Are you coming?" she said with a sheepish grin.

Graham ignored the question. Grabbing a pair of pants from her bag, she walked into the bathroom and changed. The room was empty when she walked out. She shook her head at the image of herself in the mirror and put her shoes on.

Chapter 12

The Pioneers showed up ready to play and took the lead three to two in the first inning. The second and third innings were scoreless for both teams, but the fourth and fifth innings were crazy. Both teams were getting hits and Whitney was even hit by a pitch, but it was still scoreless.

In the bottom of the sixth the other team was up and the first batter was walked. The second batter came up, showing bunt on every pitch. Graham kept watching the girl on first base move further and further from the bag so she gave the signal for a low ball in the dirt. Bailey pitched it perfectly and sure enough the girl ran. Bailey dove to the ground as Graham launched the ball to second. Dashtin ran to cover second and caught the ball, barely tagging the runner out as she slid past her.

On the next pitch the batter finally connected with the ball, bunting it down but the ball popped right up in the air. Graham caught it and rocketed it down to Whitney at first in time to get her out. With two outs, the top of the other team's batting order was up and the next batter hit the very first pitch that was thrown to her, over the fence. Graham threw her mask back and ran out to the mound.

"Damn it. I let that ball go way too early," Bailey said.

"Don't let it get to you." Graham patted Bailey on the shoulder. "She's good. She saw the ball wasn't curving and went for it, but we're better."

Graham ran back to the plate and called the next pitch. The batter swung, hitting the ball foul. She did the same thing on the following pitch allowing Bailey to get ahead zero and two in the count. Graham purposely called a ball hoping the girl would swing again, but she didn't. The girl stepped in on the next pitch and nailed it. The ball landed in the gap between center and right field. The right fielder grabbed the ball, throwing it in as hard as she could as the runner rounded second base on her way to third. Dashtin caught the incoming ball as the girl headed home and threw as hard as she could. Graham caught the ball and held her ground as the girl crashed into her. They landed in a heap near the plate with orange dust flying all around.

The umpire jumped to the side and shouted. "Out!"

That was the third out, ending the inning. The team raced in high-fiving Graham as she removed her catching gear, shaking some of the dirt out of her light blue uniform.

"That was a hell of a play," Whitney said.

"I thought for sure she was going to slide around you. I can't believe she went head-on like that," Bailey said. "Are you sure you're okay?"

Graham smiled. "I'm fine. That's what all this padding is for."

In the top of the seventh Whitney stepped up to the plate, hitting a ground ball on the second pitch. She was thrown out at first. Graham went up behind her. She watched Coach Walker's calls, but wasn't sure what the hell she was calling so she watched the ball and swung when she saw a good pitch. The bat cracked the ball sending it between second base and left field. She knew it was going to be caught but she ran as fast as she could anyway as the shortstop and left-fielder collided trying to get the ball.

Helena slapped her ass yelling, "Go!"

Graham was caught off guard and ran to second, sliding to the base just before the girl caught the ball to tag her out.

Dashtin stepped out of the batter's box swinging the bat a few times before stepping back in. She swung at the first pitch, hitting it foul. She checked her swing on the next pitch that was called a strike. She stepped forward in the box and smacked the bat against the next ball, sending it soaring to the left field fence. Graham ran around third and crossed home plate. Dashtin dove for third base as the third base player caught the ball. Dashtin was called out and Coach Walker stormed up to the umpire.

"Are you kidding me with this? You need your eyes checked. She was on that bag way before that girl caught the ball and you damn well know it! This is bullshit," Coach Walker was in his face yelling. Coach Parker pulled her back to the dugout before she got ejected from the game.

The team was still up by one with Katie up next to bat and Bailey behind her. Katie hit the first pitch straight to the second base player in a line drive for an out that nearly took the pitcher's head off.

The Pioneers took the field once again. Graham ran to the mound along with Dashtin.

"Three outs," Dashtin said. She and Graham touched gloves before she ran back to her position.

"Three up and three down." Graham winked and smiled at Bailey.

The first batter struck out after five pitches. The second batter hit a ground ball past third that rolled over the foul line too late. She ran like her ass was on fire to cross first and slid into second before the third base player could field the ball. The next batter hit a ground ball that Dashtin caught and threw to first. Whitney caught the ball at first as the girl crossed the bag and the umpire called her safe, saying Whitney's foot wasn't on the bag.

Coach Walker stormed out of the dugout. "That was a bullshit call. I could see her foot on the bag from here, you blind bastard!"

"Come on, Linda. You're going to be tossed. We all know he can't see worth a shit," Coach Parker said.

Bailey let her nerves get to her and threw a few pitches that were definitely out of the strike zone and on a three and one count the next pitch was in the sweet spot curving into the batter as it neared the plate. The umpire called it a ball allowing the batter to take a base which loaded the bases.

Graham ran out to the mound. "They're playing dirty. Just pitch around this next one. She's a slap hitter that will probably strike out," she said before running back to the plate.

The girl slapped the first ball foul and swung for a strike on the second pitch. Graham called a screwball pitch and Bailey threw it perfectly. The batter stepped right into the pitch causing it to hit her. The umpire yelled for her to take the base which meant a runner came in, scoring the winning run for the other team.

"She stepped over the plate! That's a fucked up call," Graham yelled at the umpire behind her. "Cheating pieces of shit!"

"You can bet we will be protesting this game, you cheating son of a bitch," Coach Walker said to the umpire as she and Coach Parker pulled Graham out of his face before she hit the old blind toad.

The Pioneers lined up to shake the other team's hands respectfully and boarded the bus with their heads hung low.

"We played our hearts out today and the other team intentionally cheated and the head umpire was obviously biased. I'm as pissed as you all are, but there's not much we can do about it except move on and hopefully run them into the dirt in tomorrow's game," Coach Walker said.

"I don't know about you, but I'm beyond pissed," Dashtin said to Graham who was next to her, staring through the window.

"I've never wanted to hit an umpire before," Graham said without turning her head.

"At first, I thought you did hit him when I saw both coaches running towards you," Whitney said.

"His blind ass would've been on the ground if I'd hit him," Graham said shaking her head. "That was just an all around shitty game."

"We'll get them tomorrow," Vanessa said. "I hope Bailey will be able to pitch. They wore her out."

"She will probably start so she can come back in, but Sarah will probably pitch tomorrow," Graham said.

"You two sure are getting chummy," Dashtin said.

Graham finally turned away from the window and looked at her best friend. "She's pitching better isn't she?"

"Yeah, actually she is. What did you do to her?" Whitney asked.

Graham's mind drifted to the numerous things she'd done to Bailey in the last twenty-four hours. "Nothing," she said. "We've been working together a lot on her pitching and it seems to be paying off. She has better ball control so less of her pitches are going wild."

Dashtin looked at Graham but didn't comment.

The bus pulled into the hotel and everyone piled out, walking into the hotel without retrieving their gear from the bus. There really was no need since they had another game the next day anyway.

"Dinner is at seven," Coach Walker said in the lobby.

Graham boarded the same elevator with Whitney, Dashtin, Claudia, and Bailey.

"I personally think we should be allowed to order room service and a few alcoholic beverages after the day we've had," Whitney said.

"I agree," Dashtin said.

"We can't drink on the road and Coach Walker wants everyone together as a group for dinner," Graham said.

"I keep forgetting you're such a saint, Captain," Dashtin countered. "I expect you to be on time for dinner."

Graham rolled her eyes. "I bet I'm down there before you."

"I'll take that bet. How about whoever doesn't show up on time has to pay all of next month's rent," Dashtin said.

"You're on," Graham said, shaking her hand.

The elevator doors opened and everyone disbursed to their rooms.

"What's with the rent bet?" Bailey asked as she and Graham walked into their room.

"We both hate losing so we bet on things. I usually win. Dashtin's had to wash the dishes for a month, do my laundry for a month, all kinds of other things. She insists on betting," Graham shrugged, kicking off her shoes as she began removing her gritty uniform. She noticed Bailey watching her so she casually removed each piece until she was naked before turning and walking into the bathroom and starting the shower.

Bailey waited until the water was running before stripping her uniform and joining her.

"Oh no you don't," Graham said.

"Come on, we can shower faster this way."

"That's actually not true," Graham said, watching Bailey shampoo her hair while she lathered herself with soap.

Graham was just about to turn the water off when Bailey pushed her back against the cool tile wall.

"I do believe I owe you something," Bailey said, sliding her fingers between Graham's legs through the wetness she knew was there.

Graham groaned. It felt too good to stop her. She hoped the hot water didn't run out as Bailey ran her fingers back and forth then in circles over and over again while licking and sucking the slippery wet breasts in her face.

Graham bent her head to meet Bailey's mouth for a slow sensual kiss, taking the time to nibble her bottom lip before licking.

"Spread your legs," Bailey said, breaking the kiss.

Graham obeyed, praying she didn't lose her balance and crash them both to the floor when Bailey pushed her fingers inside of her. She slid them in and back out again to rub more circles before dipping back inside, deeper each time. Graham had one arm around Bailey's wet body and the other gripping the shower rail, holding on for the ride.

Bailey ran her teeth over Graham's neck and down her chest to her breasts before kissing her way back up to Graham's mouth. She pulled her hand away when Graham began to tighten around her fingers.

"Don't stop," Graham said, gasping through gritted teeth.

Dropping to her knees, Bailey plunged her tongue inside of Graham, sucking her into her mouth at the same time. Graham put her hand in Bailey's hair, holding the back of her head as she rode her face until there was nothing left. Breathlessly, she pulled Bailey back up to her, kissing her deeply. The taste of herself on Bailey mouth made her wet all over again.

"We have to get out of here before we freeze to death," Graham said, realizing the water had gotten a lot cooler.

Bailey laughed and stepped out while Graham turned off the water. All of a sudden, they heard banging on the door.

"Son of a bitch," Graham said.

She threw on clothes as fast as she could and towel dried her hair as much as possible before going to the door. Whitney and Vanessa were standing in the hallway with their hands on their hips.

"What's wrong?" Graham asked.

"We've been knocking for ten minutes. I even called you like three times. We were about to go get someone to open the door for us, thinking you were dead," Vanessa said.

"I was in the shower," Graham said.

"I see you found her," Dashtin said, walking towards them from her room down the hall.

"What's going on?" Bailey asked. She was standing behind Graham towel-drying her hair.

"Coach said we could order some pizzas instead of having dinner here so we were checking to see who was in," Whitney said.

"Did you two shower together?" Vanessa asked with a raised eyebrow.

"Sure looks like it to me," Dashtin sneered.

"What?" Graham shook her head no. "I showered and as soon as I got out she got in and I guess I didn't hear you knocking while I was getting dressed."

"Where was she while you were showering?" Dashtin asked.

"On the phone," Bailey said. "I guess I didn't hear the knocking either."

"The pizzas will be here any minute. We ordered you one anyway," Dashtin said before turning and going back to her room.

Whitney shrugged and followed her.

"I'll call you when it's here. Answer your damn phone this time," Vanessa said.

Graham shut the door and smacked her forehead on it as Bailey laughed.

"It's not funny," Graham chided.

"Oh come on, Graham. Dashtin knows. She's not stupid."

"No one knows and they don't need to."

"Why keep it a secret? We're both adults. Unless, you lied to me about you and Dashtin," Bailey said.

Graham turned around to face her. "I've never lied to you. Dashtin and I are best friends that's all. She's pissed because she thinks you're a young straight kid that's going to play me."

"Well, she doesn't know me then," Bailey stepped closer to her. "What do you think?"

"Hell, I don't know anything anymore. I'm sleeping with an eighteen year old and sneaking around like I'm in high school."

"I'm nineteen and this is definitely not high school," Bailey growled and stormed over to the chair next to the window and sat down. Graham put her shoes on and left the room.

"Trouble in paradise?" Dashtin asked when she saw Graham walk into the lobby.

"Don't start, Dash," Graham said, plopping down next to her on the couch.

"I know you're fucking her. I think it's a huge mistake."

"Can we agree to disagree on this?"

"So you're admitting it then?"

"Yes. Okay, yes, we're sleeping together. I don't know where it's going. It just happened this weekend. I don't need you giving me shit about it," Graham ran her hands through her hair and sighed.

"I knew she was going to go after you,"

"Dash," Graham warned.

"Fine. Just don't get mad when I said I told you so."

"I don't say anything about the handfuls of girls that walk in and out of your life without you even knowing their names, so just this once cut me a little slack."

"I don't want to see you get hurt," Dashtin said.

"I'm a big girl. I can handle it," Graham said, watching the pizza guy come through the doors with close to a dozen pizzas.

"Hey dude, over here," Dashtin yelled, jumping up to pay him. Graham helped her carry the boxes.

"Do you think you can keep this a secret and be civilized around Bailey?"

"If she breaks your heart I'm going to tear her head off."

Graham raised an eyebrow.

"Okay," Dashtin sighed. "I'm not happy about it, but I'm a big girl too."

"Good, let's all pile in your room to eat. I don't want mine smelling like pizza."

"No you'd rather it..."

"Oh don't even go there," Graham laughed, bumping shoulders with her.

Chapter 13

Graham was surprised to see most of the team when she walked into Dashtin and Whitney's room. Bailey and Claudia were sitting at the table by the window. Some girls were on the beds while others were in chairs they'd brought from their own rooms.

"We went down to the vending machine and got a pile of drinks while you were gone," Whitney said as she pointed at the bathroom where the soda cans and water bottles were in the sink on ice.

"Help yourselves," Dashtin said, setting the boxes on the dresser by the TV.

Every girl grabbed slice after slice, eating carelessly until there was nothing left. Graham was sitting in a chair near one of the beds playing poker with Dashtin, Whitney, and Vanessa while some of the girls were watching a movie. Bailey walked across the room to the bathroom and Graham watched her out of the corner of her eye. It was hard not to watch her. The girl was beautiful and had the sexiest body Graham had ever seen.

Dashtin kicked her in the shin, raising her eyebrows when Graham turned towards her.

"I think I'm going to bow out, ladies. I need my beauty sleep," Graham said.

"You're just leaving because we're taking all of your money," Whitney teased.

"Well, that's true too. I guess I'm off my game tonight." Graham was used to winning when they had their usual poker nights. She said goodnight and walked back to her room.

Graham kicked her shoes off, tossed her bra on top of her open suitcase, and opened her laptop. She really needed to be working on her research. Her thesis wasn't going to write itself. But, her mind kept wandering back to Bailey. She managed to read a few pages of documentation before putting the computer away. She scrolled through the handful of channels until she found something worth watching and settled into her bed.

Bailey was surprised to see Graham fast asleep when she walked in. She quietly brushed her teeth and changed clothes before slipping into her own bed.

~

The next morning, Graham woke up tossing and turning trying to shake off the fuzziness of the bad dream she was having. The sun was shining through the slats of the window blinds. Graham kicked the covers off and stretched. That's when she noticed Bailey curled into a small bundle, asleep in the middle of the bed next to her. She sat on the edge of her bed watching Bailey sleep. She looked so young and innocent with her eyes closed and her wavy dark hair spread over the pillow behind her.

"Take a picture. It'll last longer," Bailey said with a sleepy southern drawl.

Graham shrieked, jumping off the bed like something had just bitten her. "You scared the hell out of me," she said when she finally realized Bailey was actually awake and not some poltergeist.

"Serves you right." Bailey kicked the covers off, sitting up.

Graham walked over to the edge of Bailey's bed and sat down next to her.

"I told Dashtin."

"That makes sense."

"What do you mean?" Graham asked.

"She kept giving me these looks all night, especially after you left. She hates me and I think it's funny."

"Bailey, she doesn't hate you. She's looking out for me."

"What does she think I'm going to do to you?"

Graham shrugged. There was no reason to dredge up the past. "I've told you before. She thinks you're a straight girl who's playing games."

"She doesn't know me from Adam so that's bullshit," Bailey growled and moved to get off the bed but Graham grabbed her arm, pulling her back.

"I like you when you're feisty," Graham said, pulling Bailey down on top of her.

Bailey grinned, rolling her eyes as she gave in. kissing her passionately. Graham parted her legs, settling Bailey between them so she could roll her over easily.

"Oh no you don't," Bailey said pinning Graham's arms above her head and maneuvering so that she was straddling her. She rubbed her hips slowly back and forth over Graham's, teasing her with soft kisses, pulling away before the kiss could go deeper.

"Are you trying to drive me crazy?" Graham said.

"You already do that to me. I'm just returning the favor," Bailey whispered in her ear.

Bailey's smaller body was strong, but no match for Graham. She jerked her hips, rolling Bailey onto her back. Bailey was taken off guard as Graham reached down between them sliding her fingers into Bailey's panties through her wetness and directly inside of her.

Bailey's breath hitched and she jerked before spreading her legs further, settling her hips into a rhythm matching each thrust of Graham's fingers. Graham pulled her fingers away, sitting up at the same time. She put her wet fingers over Bailey's mouth and smiled when she tried to speak. Bailey snaked her tongue out, licking the fingers before she moved them away, pulling Bailey's shirt over her head and her wet panties down her legs. Bailey mirrored her, taking Graham's clothes off.

Without saying a word, Graham laid Bailey back down. She licked and kissed her stomach and breasts moving back to her lips before sliding her fingers back inside.

"You feel so good inside of me," Bailey panted in her ear as Graham kissed her neck. She pushed her hips down as hard as she could onto Graham's hand.

Graham quickened the pace, thrusting her fingers fast and hard. Bailey moaned loudly digging her short nails into Graham's back as Graham licked her breasts, sucking her nipples.

"Oh shit," Bailey said loudly when her phone went off.

Graham raised an eyebrow and lifted her head.

"We have to be at breakfast in ten minutes."

"Should I be worried you set your alarm that late?"

"Graham!"

Graham grinned. "You better come then," she said, slowing her strokes as she pressed her thumb into the wet folds, massaging Bailey's clit with every thrust of her fingers.

Bailey kissed her, moaning into her mouth and panting with every movement of Graham's fingers. She wrapped her legs around Graham, arching her back and squeezing hard as her body began to release the tension building deep inside.

Graham felt the muscles tighten around her fingers and the warm wet liquid flowed into her palm as Bailey panted heavily, riding the waves of orgasm. She reached down, pushing Graham's hand away when she couldn't take it anymore.

~

There was no time for a shower as Bailey and Graham whore-bathed and dressed quickly. They ran down to the elevator, willing it to go faster. They walked into the dining room with less than a minute to spare with all eyes on them. Graham's short hair was normally messy and sticking out so it didn't look all that much different and Bailey's was a tangled mess held back in a ponytail.

"Yeah, that's not obvious," Dashtin said, rolling her eyes. Graham ignored her as she and Bailey got in line at the breakfast bar.

"We slept in," Graham said when Whitney looked at her with a raised eyebrow.

"I forgot to set my phone," Bailey shrugged.

They both filled their plates with pancakes, sausage, fruit, and toast. Graham poured herself a cup of coffee loaded with sugar and put a chocolate milk on her plate before going to Whitney and Dashtin's table. Bailey grabbed an orange juice and walked in the opposite direction towards Claudia and Katie.

"Hungry?" Dashtin asked, stealing a piece of toast from Graham's plate.

"Get your own toast," Graham chided. "And I'm fueling up to whip some ass today."

"Something's different with you," Whitney said.

"It's because..." Dashtin started and Graham kicked her under the table.

"I'm being overcautious. This year's almost over and I have so much going on. Plus, I want to win a championship and games like we had yesterday only frustrate me."

"You and Bailey seem to be getting along better."

"Yeah, she's not so bad once you get to know her," Graham said.

"I bet," Dashtin muttered.

~

The Pioneers came out swinging hot bats, scoring five runs in the first two innings and Bailey was throwing her first college level no-hitter. The third and fourth innings went by hitless for both teams.

Sarah, the backup pitcher was up first in the fifth inning. She struck out, bringing the top of the lineup with Whitney to bat. She hit a ground ball past third allowing her to get on first. Vanessa and Katie both got hits, loading the bases. Dashtin was up next. She swung away for two strikes before connecting with the ball, sending it all the way to the fence in right field. Whitney ran home easily and Vanessa followed, sliding in time to tag the plate before the catcher caught the ball, putting the Pioneers up seven to zero.

With Katie sitting on third and Dashtin at second, Graham stepped up to the plate. She thought she was going to be walked when the pitcher threw the ball in the dirt twice, then way out of the strike zone. Graham bent her knees to get under the next pitch hitting it hard enough to sail over the first baseman's head, hitting the ground behind her and rolling over the foul line. She ran for the ball as Katie crossed home plate. The Pioneers cheered from the dugout.

Claudia batted next, hitting a pop-up that was caught and the batter behind her struck out.

"All we need is three outs," Graham said to the team. "Bailey's on a no-hitting streak. Let's try to keep it that way."

Everyone high-fived and ran out onto the field. Bailey threw a couple of warm up pitches to Graham trying to settle her nerves.

The first batter struck out easily. The batter behind her hit the ball hard, driving it deep into centerfield. Claudia dove for the ball, catching it inches from the ground for the second out. Graham watched Bailey grab the rosin bag with her pitching hand then wipe her hand off on her pants. It was a nervous habit that got worse when she was struggling on the mound. Graham called time-out and ran out to her.

"You okay?" Graham asked.

"Yeah," Bailey said.

"That girl standing in the batter's box is just as nervous as you are," Graham said, looking into Bailey's green eyes. "You can beat her."

Bailey watched Graham run back to home plate. She took a deep breath, set her feet, read the signal, and threw the ball.

The batter sat back on the pitch which was called a strike. On the next pitch, the batter fouled the ball off the end of the bat for strike two. Graham called for a screwball and Bailey shook her head no. Then, she gave the signal for an inside curve which Bailey didn't like either. Finally, she called for a rise ball. Bailey nodded and threw the ball. The batter set her feet and swung just as the ball rose over the top of the bat at the plate for a strike and the last out, ending the game on the mercy run rule. Graham shot up off the ground and ran out to the mound.

"That was awesome," she said, picking Bailey up and swinging her around as the rest of the team piled on top of them cheering Bailey's name.

The Pioneer's quickly ran back to home plate for the traditional hand-slap with the opposing team before celebrating all the way to the bus. They had a long ride home so everyone was happy they were leaving on a positive note. They stored their gear and boarded the bus. Dashtin sat with Whitney allowing Bailey to sit with Graham if she chose which is exactly what happened. Vanessa sat across the aisle from Whitney and Dashtin with Claudia next to her at the window.

"Great game, ladies. I'm so proud of this team," Coach Walker said. "Bailey, you pitched a hell of a game and the rest of the team helped carry you to your first no-hitter. Way to go!"

~

Halfway through the ride home, Bailey fell asleep with her head on Graham's shoulder.

"Are you sure there isn't something you're not telling us?" Whitney asked, peering over the top of her seat.

"She's had a hell of a weekend. Cut her some slack guys," Graham said.

"I think you look cute together," Vanessa said.

Graham rolled her eyes. Ignoring her, she turning the volume up on the movie she was watching on her phone.

An hour later, Bailey woke up and most of the bus had fallen asleep, including Whitney and Dashtin who just happened to lean their heads together in their sleep.

Graham gestured for Bailey to get up. She put her finger over her mouth, signaling for her to be quiet. Graham walked ahead of the seats in front of hers and took a picture of Whitney and Dashtin passed out together with her phone. She smiled cheering silently as she went back to her window seat.

"Why did you do that?" Bailey whispered.

"Ammunition. Those two are a pain in my ass and this will hopefully get them off my back," Graham said.

"I wonder how passed out everyone really is," Bailey said, rubbing her hand up Graham's thigh.

Graham flinched, pushing her hand away. "Not that passed out!"

Bailey laughed.

"What am I going to do with you?" Graham shook her head.

"I can name a few things," Bailey said, biting her bottom lip.

"Oh, I bet you can." Graham grinned.

"Seriously, when will I get to see you now that we're back? Besides practice," Bailey asked.

"I'm going to be really busy over the next two months trying to get my stupid thesis done in time so I can graduate this summer, but we'll find time to see each other if that's what you want."

"Why wouldn't it be what I want?"

"Bailey, you're still in your freshman year. You have so much ahead of you here. You're beautiful. You can have any number of girls over the next three and half years."

"But I can't have you? Is that what you're saying?" Bailey said, turning in her seat to face Graham.

"No, I didn't mean it like that."

"How many girls have you dated in your four years here?"

Graham looked out the window, then back at Bailey's green eyes. "You're the sixth."

"Did you sleep with all of them?"

"No. I spent my first two years in a relationship and then dated here and there after that."

"What makes you think I want to date a bunch of girls?" Bailey asked.

"I did. Everyone wants to date as many people as possible and not be tied down, especially in their freshman year."

"I'm not everyone, Graham."

"I know that."

"What do you want? From me, I mean. Do you want to date or are you just looking to hook-up here and there? I'm confused," Bailey said.

"I do want to date you or I never would've let anything happen between us this weekend. I'm not into hook-ups and I'm not into dating multiple people at the same time either."

"Good, I don't hook-up or date around so we're on the same page."

"How many people have you dated? I mean as in a monogamous relationship?" Graham asked.

"You're number two not counting high school. I met a girl the first week I was here and we hit it off right away but she was really controlling so that didn't work out. I've dated a few girls since then, but nothing serious."

"I thought you were going to say it was Alex for a second there," Graham said.

"No," Bailey laughed. "Alex has tried everything under the sun but it's just never going to happen. She's more like my best friend, kind of like you and Dashtin. I'm still surprised you two never slept together."

Graham grimaced. "I love her to death and if I were into hook-ups I'd be all over her, but we're like oil and water and those two don't mix. We're much better off as friends."

"That's good because I want you all to myself," Bailey said, running her hand down the center of Graham's chest.

"I'm beginning to think you're a bad girl," Graham replied, grabbing her hand and moving it back to her own lap.

"Only as bad as you want me to be," Bailey teased.

Graham shook her head. "Do you have early or late classes?"

"Early."

"Me too, but I have labs three days a week that take up most of the day. Maybe we can have dinner together one night. Most of my spare time is spent doing research, but I do want to see you."

"I should tell Claudia."

"Why?"

"She's my roommate. We do a lot together. Besides, she will wonder where I am when I don't come home."

"Who said you were staying the night?" Graham teased.

"Okay, we'll see what happens," Bailey said, raising an eyebrow.

Chapter 14

The next week, Graham was sitting in her Molecular Biology of Animals Lab trying to concentrate on the rat blood cells she was looking at under the microscope. The red blood cells on the slide sent her mind drifting to Bailey, causing her to see the swirl of Bailey's green eyes instead of the swirl of red. She backed away from the table. It had only been two days since she'd seen her, but it felt like decades. Graham changed the microscope slide and tried to focus once again. She needed to compare multiple slides and make notes based on the progress of alcohol in the rats' bloodstream.

At the end of the lab course, she would need to write a paper on her study of how different amounts and types of alcohol effect rats through the bloodstream and how quickly each one slows the motor skills and at this rate she was going to be way behind. Science was Graham's passion. She loved the process of studying animal cells and organisms. This was the first time something, or in this case someone, had come between her and her passion and she wasn't sure how she felt about that.

Graham looked at the clock on the wall, shaking her head. She went back to the microscope since she had another two hours to go. She grabbed her notebook, making a few notes on the slide she was looking at and turned the microscope off. She walked over to her caged rats that the blood had been taken from. Each of the half-dozen rats assigned to her for this lab had been injected with various amounts and types of alcohol and her assignment was to watch the rats, look at their blood specimens under the microscope, and write a report on the entire study.

With an hour left on the clock, Graham picked up her phone and texted Bailey, asking her if she wanted to go to dinner. Bailey was sitting in her Macroeconomics class bored out of her mind when her phone vibrated. She smiled and quickly texted Graham back saying she would meet her at *Sister Fred's* in a few hours. She still had one more class to go and a pile of homework.

~

Graham walked through the door of her apartment and kicked off her sneakers. Dashtin was sitting on the couch with her eyes glued to the TV. Graham noticed something moving on the wall behind her head as she walked past her.

"There's a spider on the wall," she said casually.

"Where?" Dashtin screamed, diving off the couch like she was on fire.

"Good grief, Dash. It's just a spider."

"Where the fuck is it?" Dashtin said, jumping around all over the place like she was losing her mind.

"Right there," Graham said, smacking the wall with a nearby magazine. "It's gone you big pansy ass."

"I hate bugs and you know it."

"It wasn't going to get you," Graham laughed.

"Bugs are your thing not mine. I'd appreciate it if you did your homework somewhere else," Dashtin chided, going back to her seat on the couch.

"I'm not studying entomology, you nitwit. I work with rats."

"Rats, bugs, it's all the same."

Graham shook her head. "I'll bring a rat home for you tomorrow then."

"Hell, no you won't. Spiders are bad enough. We don't need rats too!"

"You know if you hadn't taken your basic biology classes when I did you wouldn't be graduating soon with a double degree in Athletic Training and Sports Science."

"Exactly. You're my nerd. Everybody in college has a 'nerd' so that they can get through the hard classes."

"I see. I guess that makes you my nitwit. Everybody has one of those too, a friend that can't find their way out of a wet paper bag without your assistance," Graham countered and ducked when Dashtin threw a pillow at her head.

"We need to trade labs. I want to spend hours a day getting rats drunk. That sounds like way more fun than rehabbing muscle weakness," Dashtin said, following Graham down the hall to her room.

"Okay, you write my twenty page report about the drunken rats and I'll go massage muscles for you."

Dashtin rolled her eyes. "Nerd," she said.

"Is there anything else you needed?" Graham asked. "I have a pile of chapters to read for my Evolution class and I don't have a lot of time."

"Hot date tonight?" Dashtin teased.

"As a matter of fact, yes I do have a date tonight."

"Have fun," Dashtin said, shaking her head. She didn't care for Graham dating Bailey and she hoped she didn't have to help her friend pick up the pieces of her broken heart again.

~

Graham pulled up at *Sister Fred's* freshly showered and dressed in a thin, long-sleeved, gray sweater and jeans. She wormed her way through the small crowd to the table in the back. Bailey was sitting alone, studying the menu.

"Hey," Graham said, sitting down across from her.

"Hi there," Bailey replied, smiling at her. "I've missed you."

"Me too."

"Only seeing you at practice sucks," Bailey said.

"I would've picked you up."

"Claudia was going this way on her way to the movies so she dropped me off."

They quickly placed their dinner order with the waitress when she stopped at their table.

"I hate not seeing you more than practice, but my schedule is so hectic right now. I only have two classes, but my labs are critical and take up most of my time. They're a huge part of my thesis."

"You hadn't told me what your thesis is. I only know you're a biology major."

"I don't talk about school much because it bores everyone to tears," Graham smiled. "I study rats. My thesis is about the biological effects of human impairment on rats and their mental state. I've studied the effects of rats that smoked pot, ingested narcotics, and now I'm studying drunken rats."

Bailey laughed. "Are you serious?"

"As a heart attack."

"That's really cool. I had no idea you were scientist smart."

"Rats gross people out and science bores them so I usually don't discuss it."

"I think it's interesting. I'm not really into science, but I'm actually taking Biological Science now. We've been learning about plant biology and next week we move on to animal biology and then human biology is last."

"Really? Aren't you a business major?"

"Yes," Bailey shrugged. "It's a general requirement and seemingly less boring than economics. If it hadn't been for you texting me I might have fallen asleep in that class today."

Graham laughed. "Well, if you want to learn about biology, I'm an open book and if you want to see it up close I can show you my rats."

"That would be cool," Bailey said smiling.

Graham studied Bailey's face. "You're the first person that has ever been interested in my study."

"I find it interesting. You're obviously smart as hell, Graham. There's no need to hide that from me."

Graham nodded and leaned back so the waitress could set their food on the table. She was thankful for its arrival because she wasn't sure what to say. They ate in silence, listening to the juke box in the corner blasting song after song.

"Do you want to dance?" Graham asked when they finished their meal.

"I thought you only dance with Dashtin?" Bailey teased.

Graham got up from the table and followed her to the dance floor. She couldn't keep her eyes off Bailey's tight ass in the jeans she was wearing. She wondered how she was going to dance with the beautiful woman in front of her without letting the entire room know how much she wanted her.

Thankfully, the song was fast, but that didn't stop Bailey from grinding against Graham, playfully rubbing her ass in her crotch. Graham held her breath, spinning Bailey around to face her. The song quickly ended and Graham grabbed Bailey's hand, pulling her from the dance floor.

"You keep dancing like that and the entire town is going to know we're together," Graham said.

"I don't see what the big deal is," Bailey said.

"I'm worried about the team. We've had a great start to our season and regionals are coming up soon. I don't want to throw a blanket over their heads."

"Is there a fraternizing policy? I don't remember reading one."

"No, not that I know of. That's probably why Helena keeps her claws out around me."

"She better never let me see them," Bailey growled.

"Easy, tiger. She knows I'm not interested," Graham said. "Do you want to get out of here?"

"What did you have in mind?" Bailey asked.

"I don't know," Graham said. She knew Dashtin was at home since she hadn't seen her yet at *Sister Fred's* so she didn't really want to go there. "Do you want to go to the lab?"

Bailey raised an eyebrow and shrugged. "Sure. I've never seen drunk rats."

"The effects of the alcohol have worn off by now," Graham laughed, tossing some cash on the table.

~

They arrived at the lab and Graham input the key-code for the security door. The locked clicked and she held the door open for Bailey.

"Are you allowed to be in here?"

"Yes, it's part of being a senior. I have a select time that I need to be in here working for my lab credit, but I can pretty much come in any other time as well, working on my research for my thesis. When you're doing a research study, time of day is another variable you have to work with," Graham said.

They walked further into the lab where long tables formed multiple rows across the large room. Two large glass cages with rats in them were on one table in each row with plastic tubes and towers for the rats to run through on the table next to the cages. The other end of the tables had scales, blood testing equipment, and microscopes.

"This is my section," Graham said, walking to the first row. "This cage is all male rats and this one next to it is all female."

"How do you tell them apart?" Bailey asked, looking at the black and white rodents.

"We write a number on each one with a permanent marker when they arrive. The males are even and the females are odd."

"That makes sense."

"I have twin females so it definitely helps to keep everyone separate."

"So, what exactly do you do here?" Bailey asked.

"Well, with the study I am working on now, I inject different types and levels of alcohol in each rat and take their blood to check the progress of the alcohol and watch them run through the play center. I take hand notes and voice recorded notes on everything and then sit down and put my notes together before leaving for the day. Each day that I'm in here I change the variables around," Graham said excitedly.

"It actually sounds like fun," Bailey replied, walking closer to the empty table next to Graham. "So you do you work right here?"

"Yeah, this is my work table for writing notes and so on since this is my row," Graham said.

Bailey ran her hand down Graham's chest, leaning in for a long kiss. Graham pulled away.

"There are cameras all over this room," Graham whispered in her ear.

"That's just my luck." Bailey laughed. "I'm really glad you brought me here, Graham. Thank you for showing me this."

"You're the first person I've ever shared any of this with. Most people look at me like I'm speaking nerd."

"I'm glad you chose me," Bailey grinned. "Is it odd that your nerd speak is turning me on?"

"Everything turns you on," Graham laughed. "Let's get out of here before you spontaneously combust."

Chapter 15

A month later, the Pioneers were riding the high of the best season they had ever had. So far the only game they'd lost was the one they were cheated out of in Washington. They were closing in fast on the middle of their season with hopes of making it to the College Softball World Series.

Graham arrived early for the Saturday afternoon game since she was already on campus checking on her rats and working on her thesis. Bailey walked into the locker room a few minutes later.

"What are you doing here so early?" Graham asked, wrapping her arms around the smaller woman, kissing her softly.

"I had a meeting with one of my professors. He's such a dickhead. I have an 'A' in his class and he seems to think I'm not participating enough. It probably doesn't help that I've fallen asleep at least three times," Bailey huffed. She leaned back in Graham's arms, pressing their hips together as she looked into her blue eyes.

Graham bent her head and kissed her hard as she backed her up against the large lockers. Both women were panting when they parted. Neither woman noticed the audience behind them until someone cleared their throat.

Graham turned around and Bailey looked up at the multiple pairs of eyes staring at them.

"Shit," Graham said under her breath.

"Lucy, you got some 'splainin' to do," Whitney said in her best Ricky Ricardo impersonation.

Bailey laughed and Graham looked like the cat that ate the canary.

"I guess the cat's out of the bag," Bailey said.

"You think?" Vanessa and Katie said at the same time.

"How long has this been going on?" Helena asked from the back of the room.

"A couple of months," Dashtin said from the doorway.

"You knew about this?" Whitney said.

Dashtin shrugged.

"Coach Walker and Coach Parker will need to be informed immediately to take whatever action is necessary," Helena said, storming out of the room.

The rest of the team trickled in followed by both coaches.

"I personally don't like it. It's bad for the team," one of the girls said.

"I don't think it's anyone's business," Graham growled.

"Well it is when you bring it into this locker room," another girl said.

"Alright, everyone calm down. Bailey and Graham, my office now," Coach Walker snapped.

Graham ran a hand through her hair and followed Bailey out of the locker room.

Coach Walker sat behind her desk with Coach Parker leaning against the wall. Bailey and Graham both stood in front of the desk.

"What the hell is going on?" Coach Walker asked.

Bailey went to speak, but Graham took the lead. "Bailey and I have been dating for a month and a half. We know it's not exactly ideal, but it just happened. We tried to keep it away from the team."

"As the captain of the team, do you think this it was a wise decision to get involved with a teammate?"

"No," Graham said. "But, it's a little late for that now."

"I have half a mind to suspend you both," Coach Walker growled, shaking her head. "But, there is nothing in the rule book about fraternizing or dating between teammates. I don't want it in my locker room or on my field. Let's get something straight right now. I don't want it anywhere around my team. What you two do in your own time is your own thing."

"Yes ma'am," Bailey and Graham said together before walking out of the room.

Coach Parker flopped down in the seat across from Coach Walker's desk.

"You have to admit they figured out a way to work together," she laughed.

Coach Walker smiled, shaking her head. "Yeah, by sleeping together. Did you see this coming?"

"No. I mean I knew they had gotten closer, but I didn't think it was *that* close," Coach Parker shrugged. "I guess I'm partly to blame. I pushed them together off the field. Hell, I even made them share hotel rooms. I thought if Bailey spent more time with Graham she would be able to control her nerves and the damn ball on the field. I thought they hated each other."

"I thought Graham and Dashtin were together for the longest time, but no one ever said anything to me so I assumed the team was okay with it. Maybe Bailey came between them," Coach Walker said.

"No," Coach Parker said. "I've heard stories around the locker room. They were definitely not together."

"I'm so confused and we have a ball game in thirty minutes," Coach Walker laughed. "What a mess."

~

Bailey and Graham went to the bullpen to warm up while the rest of the team tossed balls back and forth on the field.

"What a cluster fuck," Graham said when they finished.

"There's nothing we can do about it now." Bailey grinned. They walked back to the dugout for the start of the game.

"I don't want any of that nonsense from the locker room to carry over to this field. We are a team, we play as a team. Now, go kick some ass," Coach Walker said.

The Pioneers took the field for the top of the first inning. Bailey started off pitching nervously, and a few balls were dropped, allowing the other team to score a run. They were able to get out of the inning, but left two of their own players on base.

The next two innings weren't much better, but they held the other team back from scoring. In the bottom of the fourth, Whitney scored off a double that Katie hit, tying the game. Dashtin, Graham, and Vanessa were all hitless so far.

The fifth inning came up and the first batter on the opposing team hit a home run off a screwball pitch that Bailey threw. Graham flipped her mask back and ran out onto the mound.

"Damn it," Bailey said.

"You can't let this shit get to you. It'll be muddy for a while, but we'll get through it. You need to let the nerves go and pitch your game. The hell with them if they want to hold a grudge against us for being attracted to each other," Graham said.

Bailey nodded and Graham ran back to the plate.

She struck out the next two batters and the third one hit a pop-up that was caught. Dashtin was up to bat first at the bottom of the fifth and finally hit a ground ball passed second to get on base. Vanessa batted behind her and hit a pop-up for an out, but Dashtin was able to get to second base. Graham shook off the nerves as she stepped up to the plate. She felt like the entire team was angry with her for something she had no control over and something that wasn't their business to begin with. This fueled the fire deep inside of her.

She swung the bat as hard as she could with all of that frustration leading the way. The bat struck the ball hard enough to sting her hands as the ball sailed over the outfield fence. Graham was so shocked she stood at the plate for a half second staring at the bat in her hand before realizing she hit a two-run home run. Graham jogged the bases and was tackled at the plate by her teammates.

The last two innings went scoreless for both teams and the Pioneers won the game. No one was happier to see that game over than Bailey and Graham. They walked to the locker room together behind the rest of the team.

"What a day," Bailey said.

"Yeah, no kidding," Graham said, holding the door for her.

Coach Walker walked into the room behind them.

"That game was a nail-biter, but we pulled through when we learned how to work together out there. I know some of you disagree with some of the recent changes to the team, but I assure you it has been addressed and will not become a thorn in the side of the team as a whole. No rules have been broken, therefore it's really only a matter of morality. Whether you agree or disagree doesn't matter. Let's take this win as a positive ending to the situation and move forward," she said before leaving the room.

"Easier said than done," one girl muttered when the coach was gone.

Graham pulled a chair into the middle of the room and stood up on it.

"As the captain of this team, and as far as I know *I* am still the captain, what is going on in any of our personal lives is just that, it's personal. It just so happens that two people on the team happen to share the same personal life. Get over it and move on. We're here to play softball for the Pioneers as a team, not roll around in each other's business, airing dirty laundry.

"In case you didn't notice, Bailey pitched a hell of a game despite being nervous and frustrated by the comments from her teammates and I hit a game winning home run. So, the two people most of you are so mad at won the damn game for you today," she growled. "We're all adults here. Grow up and act like you belong in college. This isn't high school, ladies." Graham jumped down and slammed her locker closed.

Bailey followed Graham out of the locker room.

"I think you got their attention," Bailey said, smiling as she climbed into the Jeep.

Graham laughed. "I was so pissed, I thought I might knock one of them out."

"They'll get over it. I can't believe it hasn't happened before."

"I'm sure it has, just not with this group," Graham said, driving out of the parking lot. "Am I taking you to the dorm?"

"Yeah, I wanted to celebrate the win, but honestly I'm tired," Bailey exclaimed.

"I'm tired too. I'll probably go to the lab anyway," Graham said as her phone vibrated. She pulled up to the stop sign still on campus and read the text. "Dashtin's going over to Whitney's to play cards. Do you want to come home with me?"

"I'm dirty and sweaty and not the good kind," Bailey responded.

Graham laughed. "I didn't say you couldn't use my shower," she said, turning her signal on and driving in the opposite direction of the dorm buildings.

Chapter 16

Graham showered quickly and sat on the couch in the living room while Bailey showered. She had just about dosed off watching a movie when Bailey climbed into her lap, straddling her.

"Who said you could sleep?" Bailey teased, biting Graham's lower lip before kissing her.

Graham ran her hands under the shorts she'd lent to Bailey using their larger size to her advantage as she squeezed Bailey's ass. Bailey lifted up slightly allowing Graham to move her fingers lower to the wetness surrounding her opening. She moved her hips slowly over the fingers touching her.

Graham ran one hand up and down Bailey's back, under her loose shirt. She moved her other hand around to the front of Bailey, sliding it through the wetness, burying her fingers deep inside in one swift motion. Bailey moved down on her hand, pushing her deeper before rising up and pushing back down. Graham kissed her slowly, matching the rhythm as Bailey rode her fingers.

"You feel so good," Bailey moaned into her ear.

Graham moved to the side, laying Bailey on her back careful not to remove her fingers as she lay on top of her. Bailey wrapped her legs around Graham, moving her hips up to meet every thrust of her fingers. Graham hated having clothes between them, but Bailey was close. She didn't want to stop her to remove their clothes. Instead, she slowed her fingers and kissed her, matching the strokes of her tongue with the deep penetration of her fingers.

Bailey arched her back under Graham, digging her heels into the couch cushion. "Harder, baby," she said breathlessly as her body began to tighten around Graham.

Graham pushed her fingers faster and harder until Bailey let out a guttural moan and collapsed under her panting. Graham removed her fingers and wiped the sweat from Bailey's brow with her other hand.

"I like you like this," Graham said, smiling.

"Like what?" Bailey whispered still breathing heavily.

"Sweaty, out of breath, and freshly satisfied," Graham said, kissing her. "It's a very sexy look for you."

"Oh, really?" Bailey smiled.

"Yes, in fact that's how you look when I fantasize about you," Graham wiggled her eyebrows.

"Is that so? We may need to recreate those fantasies then," Bailey moved her hips against Graham.

"We should probably move to my bed before Dashtin comes home. I'd never hear the end of it she found us like this," Graham said, sitting up and moving off of Bailey.

Bailey shrugged. "I honestly don't care what she thinks," she replied, taking the hand Graham offered to her.

Graham pulled Bailey into her room and shut the door. She casually turned the lock just in case and walked over to Bailey who was sitting on her bed. The sun was going down, casting a low light across the room. Graham climbed up onto the bed lying on her side behind Bailey.

Bailey stood up, pulled the T-shirt over her head and pushed the shorts to the floor before climbing on the bed. Graham sat up allowing Bailey to remove her shirt before pulling her shorts off. Bailey pushed Graham back down. Spreading her legs, she licked her wet folds softly before sliding her body along Graham's, kissing her way to her mouth. Graham kissed her hard, pressing her hips up into the smaller woman. Bailey reached down between them, running her fingers in lazy circles around Graham's throbbing wet center, teasing her entrance with every pass of her fingers.

Graham's breath hitched. She was already climbing the walls from touching Bailey. It wouldn't take much to send her over the edge and Bailey knew it. She slowed her movements, dipping the tip of her fingers inside pushing them in deeper and back out with every circle of her clit.

"Are you going to make me beg for it," Graham gasped.

Bailey kissed her slowly, running her tongue over her lips and sucking her bottom lip into her mouth, biting gently before releasing it as she slid her fingers deep inside of Graham.

Graham moaned, running her hands through the wavy hair cascading over Bailey's back and pushing her hips up into her. They rocked together back and forth with Bailey pushing her fingers in and out, matching the thrust of Graham's hips against her as Graham's body tightened. She tried to pull her fingers out but Graham grabbed her.

"Stay inside," She said, kissing Bailey and holding her until the spasms in her body stopped. She relaxed allowing Bailey fingers to slip free.

Bailey moved to the side and kissed her cheek. They both froze when they heard the front door.

"Graham?" Dashtin called walking down the hallway.

"She doesn't know you're here," Graham whispered getting out of the bed. She tossed the clothes Bailey was borrowing to her and put her own clothes back on. She waited for Bailey to dress before opening the door.

"Hey, I was..." Dashtin stopped mid sentence when she saw Bailey standing behind Graham in the doorway. "What's she doing here?"

"Do I question your house guests?" Graham said.

"Whatever, I guess she should know too. When you guys left, Helena said she was going to the President of the University about the two of you. Graham, she said as a senior and the captain of the team it is morally and ethically wrong and you should be kicked off the team."

"She's just jealous because she wants to hook-up with me," Graham spat.

"What a bitch!" Bailey said.

"Oh well, Coach Walker already told us it's not against the NCAA rules," Graham said.

"It might not be, but if the school rules have a policy in place you could both be kicked off the team. She said it may go before a board of your peers to decide."

"Dash, she's full of shit and grasping at straws because she's mad. I'll talk to Coach Walker tomorrow before the game," Graham said.

"Look, I'm not thrilled you two got together, but you're my best friend, Graham and I don't want to see you get hurt in all of this. Whitney and Vanessa have both of your backs and so does Katie and Sarah. Helena's comments have them nervous. They were calling the rest of the team when I left. A lot of the players aren't happy about you two hooking up, but no one wants to see either of you kicked off the team."

"It will blow over in a week or two if we just play our games like the team we are and move on with our lives," Graham said.

"I hope you're right," Dashtin said. "I'm going to order Chinese if you're hungry."

"I'm starving," Bailey said.

Dashtin shook her head and walked down the hall to her room.

"You're staying the night, right?" Graham asked Bailey.

"Yes, unless you plan to drive me home."

"Nope," Graham said, shaking her head and smiling.

~

Graham wasn't used to someone sleeping in her bed. She woke in the middle of the night when she bumped the warm body next to her. The moonlight shining through the blinds cast a soft glow across the room allowing her to see Bailey asleep on her back. Graham lay on her side watching her. Bailey looked so peaceful in her sleep and very young and innocent. She knew she felt very strongly towards Bailey, but she was reluctant to admit she was falling for the young woman. There were too many variables in both of their lives at the moment to consider forever together, but lying there in that bed next to her at that moment she felt feelings that she hadn't felt in a long time, if ever.

Graham noticed Bailey's chest rising and falling a little faster. Her face twitched and she bit her bottom lip between her teeth. Graham wondered if she was having a bad dream and thought about waking her. That's when she noticed the covers moving suspiciously. She pulled the blanket and sheet away to see Bailey touching her naked body with one hand and pleasuring herself with the other.

"You like watching me, so I thought I'd give you something to watch," Bailey said.

"Oh, you're bad," Graham said, shaking her head.

"Shall I continue?"

"By all means," Graham answered, kicking the rest of the covers to the floor.

Bailey squeezed her breast with one hand, pinching her nipple between her fingers. The fingers of her other hand were rubbing her clit back and forth in slow circles. She arched her back slipping her fingers inside, coating them with wetness before pulling them back out to continue the circles.

Graham had never seen anything as erotic as watching a beautiful woman pleasure herself in her bed.

She listened to Bailey's breath hitch as she watched her hands on her body. She too was naked and having a very hard time not touching herself. She felt like she was turning inside out as her center throbbed and the wetness pooled between her legs.

Bailey dug her heels into the bed, moaning softly as her body began its release. She tightened around her fingers as she pushed them inside one last time, riding the pulsing orgasm as it washed over her. She pulled her fingers free, rolling herself on top of Graham, kissing her hard before her own body could relax and recover. Graham ran her hands down Bailey's back to squeeze her ass and back up again, massaging the muscles along her spine as they kissed.

Graham moved her mouth, kissing Bailey's neck and shoulder then moving back to the soft spot behind her ear. Bailey rocked her hips against Graham's searching for her lips. She kissed her tenderly and pulled away, sitting up to straddle Graham's waist. She looked into Graham's blue eyes and grinned before turning around. She spread Graham's legs lying back down with her hips hovering over Graham's mouth as ran her tongue over the wet folds between Graham's legs.

Graham groaned at the contact and pulled Bailey down onto her mouth. They settled into an easy rhythm, matching each other stroke for stroke. Graham was so close already from watching Bailey. She moved her hips back and forth, guiding Bailey's tongue where she needed it most as she licked and sucked her in return.

Unable to hold off any longer Graham moaned as quietly as possible, digging her fingers into Bailey's back as her body thrashed wildly causing Bailey to let go with her. They rode the waves together, gasping and moving back and forth uncontrollably until they were both completely spent. Bailey rolled over on her back breathless.

"I think you're trying to kill me," Graham whispered when she finally caught her breath.

Bailey laughed. Turning around, she kissed Graham softly, curling into her arms.

Chapter 17

Two weeks later, Graham was sitting in the lab watching her intoxicated rats trying to navigate the plastic tunnel system. She'd just taken blood from each one, recording the last results of the days test on alcohol in the bloodstream in her laptop. She almost missed her phone ringing because it was buried in the bottom of her laptop bag.

"Hey," she said, surprised to see Bailey's name on the caller ID.

"Claudia and I were in an accident. Some asshole ran a red light and hit us," Bailey said.

"Oh my god, are you okay?"

"Yeah, we're both banged up. They took us to University Hospital. My pitching shoulder is really sore from the seatbelt and being slammed into the side of the door. They just did an x-ray."

"I'm in the lab so I'm close by. I'll be there in a few minutes," Graham exclaimed, hanging up the phone. She tore off her lab coat, closing her laptop at the same time. She packed up quickly and took off out the door.

~

Graham arrived at the hospital within a few minutes. The nurse at the desk said Bailey was having tests done and they would let her know when she could be seen so she asked about Claudia. They allowed Graham to go back to the ER to see her while she waited for Bailey.

"Hey, how are you feeling?" Graham said, pushing the curtain aside.

"I'm okay," Claudia sighed. "I have some bruises and cuts and scrapes from the glass. I think they are going to release me in a few minutes."

"Is someone coming to get you?"

"Rayjay is coming to get me," she replied.

"Rayjay? As in Rayjay Mathis the star football player?" Graham asked.

Claudia smiled. "Yeah, he and I are dating."

"Is he a sophomore or a junior?"

"Sophomore. He's so sweet. He has all these plans to take care of me. I tried to tell him I'm okay. How is Bailey? Have you seen her?"

"No, she was having tests done when I got here. Her shoulder is banged up pretty good, but she's okay."

Claudia shook her head. "That guy must have been texting on his phone or talking or something. We were riding along and all of a sudden...BAM! He never even hit his brakes. He hit us just behind Bailey's door near the rear tire. He probably would've really hurt her badly if he had hit her door."

"Was he okay?"

"Yeah, he was walking around with his arms in the air, talking on his phone while the EMT's had to help Bailey get out of the car. My side was fine so I opened my door and got out, but she was in pain and had a hard time climbing over the console."

"Excuse me," the nurse said to Graham. "Miss Michaels is back from her tests. She's down at curtain three if you want to see her."

"Tell her I'm sorry," Claudia said.

"It's not your fault. You go home with Rayjay and get some rest. You'll be sore tomorrow. I already called Coach Walker. She will probably check on you later," Graham said before walking away.

"Aren't you a sight for sore eyes," Bailey said when Graham pulled the curtain back. She winced in pain as she tried to adjust her position on the gurney.

Graham walked over to her and kissed her lips softly as she reached down and grabbed her hand. Bailey held her hand tightly.

"How bad is it?"

"I don't know. I just had an MRI. The doctor said the x-ray didn't show any broken bones but there was a lot of tissue swelling so he ordered the MRI to see if there's a tear. They just gave me some pain medicine in my IV so hopefully that helps soon."

Graham rubbed her thumb over the top of Bailey's hand. "Do you want me to call your family?"

"I called my mom after I talked to you. She was ready to book a flight, but I told her I'm fine. I guess I will call her back once I know for sure. If there's a tear I may need surgery. There goes our winning season. We are weeks away from regionals. I'm so pissed," Bailey sighed.

"Don't worry about the softball season. That should be the last thing on your mind. I talked to Coach Walker on the way here. She sends her sympathy and told me to take care of you. She said she will check in with you tomorrow, but told me to keep her updated."

"How's Claudia?" Bailey asked.

"She's okay, just cuts and bruises. Why didn't you tell me she was dating Rayjay Mathis?"

Bailey shrugged. "I didn't know he was a star football player until I went to dinner with them last week and people were asking to take pictures with him. I mean I knew he played, but he's only a sophomore. I didn't expect him to be so popular."

"He's a hell of a running back. If he stays healthy he will probably go into the NFL."

"Wow, shows how much I know," Bailey laughed.

Both women jumped when the doctor pulled the curtain back, but Bailey held onto Graham's hand.

"Miss Michaels, the MRI shows a lot of swelling and bruising, but we do not see a tear. It looks more like a sprain. I'm going to release you, but you will need to follow up with an orthopedic specialist as soon as possible. We have a few that work with the university athletic department here in the hospital. I will make sure you get their information with your discharge papers. You need to use alternating ice and heat on your shoulder and ibuprofen will help with the pain and swelling."

"Yes, sir," Bailey said. She looked up at Graham when he left the room.

"I think you should come home with me and let me take care of you," Graham said.

"I need to go by my place and get some clothes. As much as I love wearing yours, they're a little big and I will need clean underwear. I also need to call my parents," Bailey said.

"You can call them now if you want. I'm going to go out in the hall and call Coach Walker. I'll be back in a few minutes to get you," Graham said.

~

Dashtin was sitting on the couch watching the TV when Graham walked in with Bailey. She jumped up to grab the door since Graham's hands were full with Bailey's bag and her computer bag.

"How are you feeling?" Dashtin asked.

"Really sore," Bailey said, sitting on the couch.

Graham handed Bailey's release papers to Dashtin as she walked by her. She placed her computer bag on the desk in her room and put Bailey's bag on her bed.

"I have some ice packs in the freezer and a heating pad," Dashtin said as she read the notes from the hospital. "If it's as swollen and bruised as they said it was they won't see a tear for a day or two. The best thing you can do is to try not to move it a whole lot and go see Dr. Farris tomorrow. He's one of the best ortho doctors. He lectured one of my classes last year."

"Dashtin's is an athletic training major with a sports medicine minor," Graham said.

"And I thought you were the nerd," Bailey said, smiling at Graham.

"Ask her who did all of her science homework," Graham said.

"What did Coach Walker say?" Dashtin asked.

"Not much. She said to follow up with the doctors and when she's cleared you can work with her to try and get her throwing again slowly so she doesn't injure herself."

"I figured as much. How's Claudia? You said she didn't get hurt, right?"

"I just talked to her," Bailey said. "She has some cuts from the glass smashing and some bruising from hitting the console with her side, but she's fine."

"Are you going to practice?" Dashtin asked Graham.

"Yeah, I'm sure Coach Parker wants Sarah working her arm for the rest of this week so she can pitch this weekend," Graham said. "Do you want me to make you some macaroni and cheese or something before I go? We don't have any soup," she said to Bailey.

"No, I'll be fine. They gave me some medicine before we left so I have a few hours. I think I'm just going to lie down for a while," Bailey said.

"Go get into my bed. It's more comfortable than this lumpy old couch." Graham kissed her softly. "I'll see you in a couple hours. Call me if you need anything."

"Do you want to ride together? I'm not doing anything afterwards," Dashtin said.

"Might as well," Graham said. "Let me change clothes real quick." She ran down the hall and changed into her warm-up pants, a T-shirt, and sneakers.

~

Graham went through the motions at practice, but her mind was miles away. Sarah wasn't a bad pitcher. In fact, her ball control was precise, but she lacked the speed and pop that Bailey put on the ball when she threw it. Graham just about let the ball hit her in the face a few times because she wasn't paying attention.

After close to an hour, Coach Parker sent them both to the batting cages to finish their practice. Graham swung the bat, connecting with a few of the balls, but most of them sailed past her head. The coaches ended practice shortly afterwards and Dashtin and Graham hurried home instead of sticking around to talk with everyone.

"I guess that mess with Helena has blown over. I haven't heard anymore about it," Dashtin said as she drove them across campus.

"She had no grounds. Coach Walker already knew the rules and told us we didn't break any so she was just being a bitch and trying to stir something up," Graham stared out the window. 'Thanks for helping me with Bailey. I really hope it's nothing serious."

"She'll be fine. You need to get her into the doctor tomorrow though if possible. The sooner the better," Dashtin said.

Graham walked into the quiet apartment, careful not to make any noise. Bailey was asleep in the middle of her bed. She walked over and brushed the hair off Bailey's cheek as she bent down and kissed the spot softly.

Bailey stirred and winced when she opened her eyes.

"Hey baby, we just got back. I didn't mean to wake you," Graham said.

"No, it's fine. I was asleep for a while."

"Do you want me to make you something to eat?"

"Mac and cheese is fine. I'm not real hungry," Bailey said.

"Okay, do you want to try to take a shower or maybe a bath?"

"No. I did call the doctor. I have an appointment tomorrow afternoon. I also emailed my professors from my phone to let them know I was in an accident and I won't be in class tomorrow."

"You've been busy," Graham smiled.

"It was getting late and I wanted to get all of that done before the end of the day, so I did it when you left."

"I'll be right back," Graham said, turning the TV on in her room. She gave Bailey the remote before going to the kitchen.

A few minutes later, Graham returned with a large bowl of macaroni and cheese. Bailey's stomach growled indicating she was hungrier than she thought she was. Graham left her to eat while she took a quick shower.

Bailey had finished her dinner and was half asleep watching TV when Graham walked back into the room.

"That's just wrong," Bailey said.

"What?" Graham asked, looking over at her. She had dropped her towel on the floor when she entered the room and was searching her dresser for clothes.

"You're standing there naked knowing I can't do anything about it. That's just plain mean," Bailey pouted.

Graham grinned pulling on a pair of shorts and a T-shirt. She climbed into the bed next to her careful not to hurt her shoulder as Bailey snuggled against her.

"I'm sorry. I'll make it up to you when you get well," Graham said, kissing her lips.

"You better," Bailey said.

"Did your phone ring a few minutes ago? I thought I heard it when I turned the water off."

"Yeah, it was my mom. She said to call her tomorrow as soon as I finish with the doctor. She still wants to fly here, but I told her I'm in good hands. Very good hands as a matter of fact," Bailey grinned.

Graham laughed. "I'm sure that's what you said."

"It is."

"Does your family know about you?" Graham asked.

"I had a girlfriend in high school, Graham. Of course they know. They were a little shocked at first, but they realized it wasn't a phase and accepted it as it was. Do your parents know?"

"They are divorced and don't speak to each other, but yes I told them when I came home during the summer before my sophomore year. My dad said he knew all along and had no problem with it, but my mom didn't want to admit it. She hid me in the closet and refused to let me tell anyone for a few months and then I was home for the holidays and she just blurted it out at the dinner table with the entire family there," Graham said.

"Wow, that's one way to do it, I guess."

Graham laughed. "She did it to humiliate me and all it did was make her sisters laugh at her. Everyone knew I was gay from the time I was a little kid. My mother is very high up in the social circle with her nose as high in the air as it will go and my father is the complete opposite which is why they finally divorced when I was in high school. He had enough of her socialite life. She forced him to pretend that they had the perfect marriage and hang with the high rolling crowds. Don't get me wrong, my parents are well off, but my mother lives like she's a damn Kennedy. Her whole family thinks it's a joke."

"I bet that makes for interesting visits when you go home," Bailey said.

"Yeah, I usually see her, but I stay at my dad's when I go home."

"Have you ever taken anyone home with you?"

"You mean a girl?" Graham asked.

Bailey nodded.

Graham laughed shaking her head. "Hell no. I don't like being subjected to that theater performance. Why would I make someone else sit through it too? Honestly, there hasn't been anyone I thought about taking home and during the times I went home I was single so it wasn't even an option. I'm guessing your family knew your girlfriend in high school."

"Oh yeah. Sammy, that's her name, was at our house all the time. At least she was until the summer we were headed to college. She chose Texas A&M and was so pissed when I said I was going to Central Oregon. Then the next day she said she wanted to break up so she could date guys for a while."

"That's a little weird."

"Not really, you'd have to know her. She was a bit eccentric to start with and I wasn't in love with her. We were more like best friends that experimented with each other sexually. I saw her when I was home at the holidays and after only four months in college she told me she went a little wild and screwed up. I felt bad for her, but it's her own damn fault."

"In the words of my dear old grandmother, 'You seem to have your head glued on a little straighter.' Some people get to college and go nuts. It happens a lot. They do all kinds of crazy things. Three girls dropped out of my major during our freshman year after getting pregnant. At least another ten didn't come back after failing too many classes."

"My parents tolerated Sammy, but I know they never cared much for her. Now you, they would love you. In fact, they would prefer you because you would be a good influence on me. My mom knows I'm dating someone, but I haven't given her any details. She would be begging me to bring you home with me this summer if she knew anything about you," Bailey laughed.

"I don't think they want to know what kind of influence you've been on me," Graham said, kissing her.

"You better stop that," Bailey scolded, pulling away. "Don't start something we can't finish."

"We should probably go to sleep then. Do you need any more ibuprofen?"

"No, maybe in an hour or two."

"The bottle is on the nightstand next to you by your water. Wake me up if you need help getting it," Graham said, wrapping her arms around Bailey. She kissed her lips and then her forehead.

Chapter 18

The next day, the doctor looked at Bailey's x-ray and MRI results and sent her for another set since his office was in the hospital. The swelling had gone down and there was definitely no tear. He told her it was bruised and to take it easy with no softball for a week maybe two. He also said to go back to pitching slowly, stopping if she was in pain and to go to the athletic trainer for therapeutic massage to help the muscles heal.

Bailey was feeling better towards the weekend so she joined her team for their game on Friday night which they lost by two runs. Then, they barely won Saturday's game in extra innings. By Sunday the team was exhausted and Bailey was frustrated sitting in the dugout.

The Pioneers were tied with the opposing team at one run each in the sixth. It had been a long weekend and everyone was ready for it to be over. Graham was worn out from chasing foul ball after foul ball. Sarah wasn't the strikeout pitcher Bailey was and most of her pitches were hit or fouled away.

"I hate not being out there," Bailey said.

"I know. You'll be back on the mound soon," Graham replied, patting her thigh.

Katie struck out for the third out, ending the sixth inning. Graham and the rest of the team took the field. Graham pulled everyone in at the mound.

"Three outs. We can do this. Stay on point and keep your eyes on the ball," She said. Everyone high-fived and ran off to their positions.

Sarah threw the first pitch for a surprising strike. The next pitch was clearly a ball, but the batter checked her swing too far and had a second strike called. Graham prayed for the girl to strike out and sure enough on the third pitch she tried to slap it and missed for the third strike and first out of the inning. The next girl that came up hit the first pitch hard. Graham watched it sail to the fence as the girl raced to first base. Vanessa crashed into the fence diving for the ball and missed it by an inch. The runner was rounding second when Vanessa threw the ball to Dashtin who launched it home to Graham. The runner rounded third and was halfway home when Graham caught the ball. She held her ground tagging the runner out as she tried to slide by her. The next batter to the plate made a huge mistake, hitting a short pop-up for the final out.

The Pioneers ran back to the dugout cheering. They just needed to score to win the game, but it had been extremely difficult to score the entire time. Dashtin was up first and struck out, followed by Graham who did the same thing. With two outs and another potential extra inning game looming Whitney stepped up to the plate. She took a few practice swings and moved into the box.

The first pitch was a ball on the outside. She readjusted her footing and sat back on the next pitch which was a strike. The third pitch was a screwball that came in low and wide. Whitney swung the bat, connecting with the ball as hard as she could. She watched the ball drop over the fence as she ran to first base. The entire Pioneer team came out of the dugout jumping up and down, cheering as Whitney jogged around the bases. Dashtin and Graham put her up on their shoulders.

When everyone finally made their way back to the locker room Coach Walker was standing on a chair in the middle of the room. "Way to go, ladies!" she yelled. "We had a hell of a challenge this weekend and we managed to make the best of it. I'm so proud of this team and with this win today we are guaranteed a spot in the regionals. So, congratulations to everyone." She jumped down and walked over to Coach Parker. "We need Bailey back on her game by the time we start regionals or we will never get past the first round," she whispered.

Coach Parker called Bailey, Graham, and Dashtin into her office when the celebration calmed down.

"We need to have you ready to go for regionals, Bailey. Next week I want you to work with Dashtin just throwing the ball and playing catch, nothing strenuous. You two also need to work on stretching the arm out so the muscles don't shorten. Dashtin knows what she's doing and she will be in contact with Coach Walker and me every day to discuss your progress,"

"Yes, ma'am," Bailey said.

Dashtin nodded. She knew it was coming. In a couple of months she'd have her degree so she was more than prepared. She wasn't thrilled about it. At least Bailey wasn't staying with Graham any longer since she was getting better.

"Graham, you need to work with Sarah these next three weeks on her off speed pitches because her on speed pitches aren't up to par. She needs to be ready for regionals because she will be used a lot in relief as we go forward."

"I'll start tomorrow," Graham said.

All three women walked out of the coaches' office.

"I guess we won't see each other much with our separate training routines," Bailey said.

"Yeah and I am behind with my research so I'll be in the lab a lot. We'll find time when we can. The most important thing is getting you healthy and if there is anyone that can do it I know it's Dashtin. She takes what she does very seriously. She'll get you pitching like a pro again," Graham said. "Come on, I'll drive you home."

~

Two weeks into the rigorous training and exercise sessions, Bailey and Dashtin were finally starting to work together after butting heads at every turn during the first week. The fact that they didn't like each other wasn't helping matters. Dashtin stepped up the routine during the second week and started Bailey pitching slowly.

Bailey was struggling on the mound in the pitching cage. Every pitch hurt worse than the last and she was only pitching half-speed. She stopped when she could no longer take the pain.

"This is crazy. I can't do this," Bailey yelled.

"Yes you can. It's mind over matter, Bailey," Dashtin said.

"Yeah well you try to do this shit with your shoulder burning. I'm sick of being in pain." She stormed off to the locker room. Dashtin followed.

"Let's work on massaging the muscles and tendons before you ice it. Therapeutic massage can work wonders on sore muscles," Dashtin said.

"Fine," Bailey waited for Dashtin to set up the massage table in the training room next to the locker room. She took her shirt and sports bra off and wrapped her upper body in a towel.

"Lay on your back first, we'll start with the front of the shoulder," Dashtin said. She waited for Bailey to get situated on the table and covered her hands in a cold jelly-like substance that warmed when she began moving her hands over Bailey's skin, kneading the sore muscles.

"That hurts," Bailey winced.

"It will get better, just relax."

Bailey tried to clear her mind, but nothing helped. Ten minutes later, Dashtin had her roll to her stomach. The towel came open revealing the creamy smooth skin of her entire back. Dashtin massaged the muscles softly at first, working up to a much harder deep tissue massage as she moved Bailey's arm to different angles, working every part of the tender area. Eventually, the pain subsided to more of an ache than a constant throb.

"How does that feel?" Dashtin asked.

"The pain is better and it's not as tight," Bailey said. She sat up moving her shoulder around oblivious to the towel sliding down her breasts and pooling around her waist.

Dashtin was standing next to her with her hip against the table that Bailey was sitting on. Her eyes wandered from Bailey's arm to the perky round breasts and dark nipples peaking out at her. Bailey's eyes met hers and Dashtin leaned in. Their lips touched briefly and neither woman pulled away. Dashtin pushed further deepening the kiss and Bailey opened her mouth to her.

In the blink of an eye, Bailey was on her back with Dashtin on top of her, stroking her breasts and inching her hands lower. She shook the fog from her head.

"I can't do this," she said, pushing Dashtin away. "I can't believe you can." She shook her head, wrapping the towel around herself and hastily walked back to the locker room.

Chapter 19

Graham was sitting at the desk in her room, working on her thesis when Dashtin walked in and sat on the edge of her bed.

"How was practice?" Graham said, spinning around in her chair to face her.

"Fine," Dashtin said.

"Are you sure? You look like you did that time you got chased out of that woman's bed by her truck driver husband," Graham laughed.

Dashtin raised an eyebrow and shook her head. "That has only happened once thank God."

"What's up then?"

"Nothing, I'm just tired I guess. What do you want to do for dinner? Or do you have plans?"

"No plans. Bailey just called and she's not feeling well. You guys must have had a pretty difficult practice," Graham said.

"Yeah. She's pitching and it's causing her some pain. She'll be ready by the start of regionals. She'll need to be relief though until she's stronger," Dashtin stood up and walked over to the door. "I'm going to order something from that new Italian place that left a menu on the door. Do you want anything?"

"You must be tired if you're not going out. Wednesday night is your party night." Graham laughed. "I haven't even looked at that menu. Just get me lasagna or something. I need to get these next two pages edited. I'm almost finished, finally."

~

A few days later, the Pioneers had just finished their last regular season game, easily winning ten to two. They'd finished number three in their division and earned a spot in the upcoming Regional Tournament. Graham stored her gear in the locker room and talked to a few of her team mates before leaving with Bailey.

"I can't wait to have you back on the mound. Sarah's okay, but you're more of a threat with your speed," Graham said, walking to the Jeep. She held the door for Bailey and walked around to the driver's side.

"I'm looking forward to being back too. I hate just sitting and watching the game," Bailey said.

Graham moved her hand from the gearshift to grab Bailey's. "Do you want to go get something to eat and come home with me?"

Bailey looked at Graham. The streetlights casted a soft glow inside the Jeep, lighting up her face as she drove. Bailey squeezed the hand holding hers.

"Are you still feeling bad?" Graham asked. "I can just take you to the dorm if you want."

"I need to tell you something," Bailey said.

"Okay," Graham said, turning into a parking lot on campus. "What's wrong?"

"Dashtin kissed me," Bailey said. "I didn't...I didn't stop her. At least not at first."

"Are you serious?" Graham stared at her.

"Yes."

"When was this?"

"A few days ago at my practice session," Bailey said.

"What do you mean you didn't stop her at first? How far did it go? Did you sleep with her?"

"No. It didn't go that far, but it was heading in that direction. I'm sorry, Graham."

"Sorry?" Graham huffed in shock. "Why would you make out with my best friend? I almost understand why she did it, but you?"

"I was caught up in it. She kissed me and I don't know, Graham. It just happened."

"Do you want to sleep with her?"

"No. It was a mistake. It's tearing me apart. That's why I had to tell you," Bailey wiped a tear from her cheek.

Graham shook her head staring out the window. "I can't do this," she said, starting the Jeep. She turned back towards the other side of campus and stopped in the dorm parking lot.

"Can we talk about this, please?" Bailey said.

"We just did. I'm not playing this game, Bailey. Not again," Graham said, waiting for her to get out.

Bailey wiped the tears pouring from her eyes as she got out. "I don't want to lose you, Graham. I love you."

Graham sighed. "If you loved me, Bailey, you wouldn't be standing here explaining to me why and how you made out with my best friend and almost slept with her."

Bailey shut the door and watched the taillights as Graham drove away.

~

Dashtin walked into the living room with her shoes in her hand as Graham walked inside the apartment.

"It looks like you're going out on the prowl. You must be over getting turned down," Graham said, throwing her keys hard against the wooden coffee table. "Why, Dashtin? Why her?"

Dashtin hung her head in her hands.

"I should beat your ass right now," Graham growled, angrily. "How could you do this to me?"

"I'm sorry, Graham. I didn't mean for anything to happen, it just did. I regret every minute of it."

"That's not good enough," Graham paced the floor. "Why didn't you tell me? Did you think it was okay to make out with my girlfriend and then move onto the next willing participant?" she yelled. Shaking her head she said, "I'll give you credit, Dash. It must have taken balls to stab your best friend in the back."

"I'm really sorry, Graham. I never meant to hurt anyone, especially you. This was a huge mistake. I'm not even attracted to her."

"Mistake?" Graham yelled. "A mistake is dropping a ball on the field or sleeping in and missing class! This is a catastrophic fuck-up!"

"What did Bailey say?"

Graham spun around from her pacing and stared Dashtin in the eyes. "I'm assuming the truth. You made a move and she didn't stop you."

"She's right, but she did stop. She doesn't want me and I don't want her."

"After everything I went through with Olivia cheating on me and breaking my heart, how could you do this to me, Dashtin?" Graham's voice cracked and she turned away.

"I can't tell you how sorry I am. I don't know what else to say."

"You're the most careless, insensitive person I know and I'm ashamed to call you my best friend," Graham said, grabbing her keys from the table before walking out the door and slamming it behind her.

~

Graham drove to her quiet spot at the park by the river, but thoughts of the time she'd brought Bailey there flooded her mind. She drove around town finally stopping at the lab on campus. She didn't want to blow money on a hotel room, but she didn't want to go home either. The last time she felt this emotionally drained her best friend had been there to pick her back up. This time she was the cause of it. Graham had no one to turn to.

After watching her rats sleep for what seemed like hours and crying until there were no more tears to cry out, Graham realized she really had nowhere to go. She didn't want her dirty laundry aired all over campus, so going to a teammate's house was out of the question, and her father's house was hours away. She decided to go back home and sleep in her own bed.

She snuck in quietly, hoping Dashtin was either asleep or out for the night. She didn't expect her to be sitting on the couch.

"I'm sorry, Graham."

"I don't want to hear it. I honestly don't even want to talk to you or see your face," Graham said, walking past her as she went into her room and flopped down on her bed.

Chapter 20

Two weeks later, the team traveled by bus to Boise, Idaho for their Super-Regional Tournament after winning their at-home Regional tournament easily in two straight games. No words were spoken by Graham, Dashtin, or Bailey during those two games or the few practices they'd had throughout the past two weeks and now with the three of them sitting alone in different areas of the bus, a few of the team members were starting to talk. Whitney knew something was up when Dashtin asked to room with her during the week long tournament.

Graham had her headphones on with music from her playlist playing as she watched the world go by outside through the large window. She was glad to have the past few weeks behind her. No matter how hard she tried, she kept thinking of Bailey. The grueling practices didn't help matters and sharing an apartment with Dashtin was the icing on cake. The more she moped around barely eating and barely sleeping while Dashtin watched in silence only added fuel to the fire, turning her sadness into anger.

She turned her thesis in the day before the trip along with her graduate school application. Her fate was in the hands of the very same professors that had taught her everything she knew. Without a doubt she would graduate in the coming weeks, but her future was still a blur. If she didn't get into grad school at Central Oregon she planned to move closer to her father and attend Oregon or Oregon State. In the back of her mind she really hoped she was turned down so she could move on with her life and get the hell out of Bend, Oregon.

The bus finally pulled into the hotel six hours later. Graham was one of the last people off. The less time she had to stand around near Bailey or Dashtin the better. She grabbed her bag from the storage compartment outside of the bus and turned to go inside.

Coach Walker was standing nearby with her hands in the pockets of her dress slacks. She fell into step when Graham moved to walk by her.

"Can we talk for a minute, Graham?" she said.

Graham stopped walking and turned her head. Her big blue eyes were hollow and her skin seemed pale. She looked tired and physically worn down.

"Are you feeling okay?" Coach Walker asked putting her hand on Graham's forehead after getting a good look at her.

"Yes," Graham said flinching from the touch.

"Would you care to explain to me why my three star players aren't speaking to each other?"

Graham shrugged.

"You're the captain of this team, Graham. If you're not up to par then the entire team will feed off of your negative energy. You're their leader and something is seriously bothering you. I have a very strong suspicion Dashtin and Bailey are involved in whatever it is." She paused putting her hand on Graham's shoulder. "Graham, I've known you for four years. You're extremely smart, probably one of the most intelligent students I have coached in my career. In three weeks all of this will be over. You need to choose how you want it to end. I'm here if you need someone to talk to."

Graham nodded and walked away. Coach Walker shook her head, watching her leave. If she didn't know any better she'd say the kid was heartbroken. She hoped she would be able to find a way to pull it together.

Graham walked into her room. Tossing her bag on the floor, she sat on the bed to take her shoes off as the bathroom door opened. She looked up to see Bailey walking towards her. Graham jumped to her feet.

"I must be in the wrong room," she said, reaching for her bag on the floor.

"No, I'm in the wrong room. I asked Whitney to switch with me," Bailey said.

"What the hell for? Switch back."

"We need to talk, Graham."

"There's nothing to talk about, not here, not now, not ever."

"I know about Olivia and I'm not her," Bailey said.

"Who told you about her?"

"Dashtin. She's worried about you. She said you haven't eaten and you don't sleep. You haven't said a single word to me in two weeks," Bailey said. "I never meant to hurt you, Graham."

"It's a little too late for that don't you think?" Graham growled.

"What happened with Dashtin and I was unintentional. It was a huge mistake. Neither of us are attracted to each other. I didn't have sex with her or anyone else for that matter. I'm not like that. Please don't compare me to a girl who slept with multiple people behind your back and don't compare what we had to a relationship full of lies."

"It doesn't matter what it was. It's over now."

"It doesn't have to be. Talk to me, Graham," Bailey pleaded.

"Bailey, I don't even know what to say to you."

"How do you love someone so much and just turn everything off? Tell me how to let you go because I don't know how. I can't just forget everything we had, the way we made love, I don't know how you can," Bailey snapped.

"You obviously forgot all about it when you were kissing my best friend and came within inches of having sex with her," Graham yelled.

Bailey went to say something but Graham put her hand up. "Please, just go," she said quietly.

Bailey walked out the door without another word being spoken. Graham ran her hands through her hair and sighed as she sat down on the corner of the bed. She felt like the boat she was on was sinking faster than the Titanic and there were no lifeboats left.

~

The Pioneers barely won their first game of the Super Regional Tournament and struggled even worse in their second game the next afternoon. Graham and

Dashtin struck out every time they were at bat and Bailey's pitching was so off, Sarah had to come in during the fifth inning and close out the game. If it hadn't been for a late home run hit by Vanessa that also brought Katie in, they would've lost the game.

The entire team was on edge when they walked back to the bus. Coach Walker waited for everyone to sit down. The bus wasn't even out of the parking lot before she started yelling at the team, expressing her severe disappointment in the way they'd played.

"Graham, I told you when we got here as the captain of this team you needed to grab the reins on whatever is going on between you, Bailey, and Dashtin. Now, I'm telling the three of you to get over it and move on because if we have another game like we did today I can promise you we will not win by the skin of our teeth. We are potentially moving on to the World Series where we will meet the most elite teams and honestly, at the moment, we don't look like we belong in the same category," she said as the bus came to a stop in front of the hotel. "You'd better hope Wisconsin loses tonight so that we don't have to play a third game. At this point, I'm not sure we would win."

Everyone walked off the bus behind Coach Walker. Graham was one of the last players on the team to exit the bus. She walked past most of the team that was gathering in the lobby.

"What the hell is going on?" Whitney said as she passed by.

"What?" Graham said, turning around.

"There's obviously something going and it's affecting the team. We deserve to know," Whitney said.

"Bailey and I are no longer together. If you want the details ask Dashtin. She has an answer for everything," Graham said.

"Don't even go there, Graham," Dashtin growled. "Everyone makes mistakes."

"I'm sorry I'm playing shitty, Whitney, but it's really hard to pretend I care to be around my ex-girlfriend and my ex-best friend and yes I'm going to go there, Dashtin, because if you and Bailey hadn't mistakenly 'almost' slept together, none of this would be happening right now!" Graham yelled and walked out the front door of the hotel.

The majority of the team members overheard the entire conversation along with the coaches. Everyone stood speechless as Bailey ran for the elevator in tears. Dashtin followed Graham outside. All of the players rushed to the windows as Dashtin caught up with Graham in the parking lot.

"This is ridiculous. You're acting childish, Graham. I don't know how many times Bailey or I have to apologize to you before you truly realize that neither of us wanted anything to happen. It was just something stupid that occurred. I can't take it back no matter how hard I've tried to wish it away," Dashtin said. "If you want to blame someone and be pissed at someone then hate me. I started it. Bailey just reacted."

"You may have started it but she didn't stop you right away. She let it happen. You're both to blame," Graham said.

"That girl loves you, Graham, and I know you love her whether you want to admit it or not. She's not Olivia. Stop treating her like she is before you push away the best thing that has ever happened to you."

"It's mighty funny how you couldn't stand her until all of this happened."

Dashtin wanted to choke the life out of her best friend or at least slap her around a little bit. "She has called me crying her eyes out so many times I can't even count. No one knows you better than I do and she had no one else to talk to about you. Do you hear what I'm saying, Graham? You! All she talks about is you. The day all of that happened, she told me how disgusted she was with me and how ashamed she was with herself for making the biggest mistake of her life. I told her not to say anything because I knew how Olivia tore you apart and this would make you push Bailey out of your life. She didn't understand and she didn't want lies and secrets between you two so she told you." Dashtin wiped the tears that started down her face. "Damn it, Graham, you're my best friend. I can never tell you how sorry I am."

Graham turned around and walked back into the hotel ignoring the audience of team members as she went into the elevator. Helena dove into the elevator with her just before the doors shut.

"I'm sorry about everything that's going on with you. I'm here if you need someone to talk to. Maybe we can order room service tonight instead of having dinner with the team. I'm sure Coach Walker will approve it," Helena said, putting her arm over Graham's shoulders.

Bailey was sitting on the floor in front of the door to her and Claudia's room when the doors opened. Graham didn't notice her at first, she was too busy trying to get out from under Helena's claws.

"Are you kidding me?" Bailey spat. She stood up as they exited the elevator. Helena smiled at her, still holding her arm around Graham's shoulders.

"I'm going to let Coach Walker know we're going to order room service and stay in tonight," Helena said loud enough for Bailey to hear, placing her other hand on Graham's upper arm.

Graham's head was pounding. She felt like she was hit over the head with a bat and put on a rollercoaster. "What are you doing in the hallway?" she said to Bailey as she pulled away from Helena's grasp.

"Claudia has the room key," Bailey's face was still wet from tears. "What are you doing with her?"

Graham looked at Helena. "You can tell Coach Walker I'm ordering room service tonight if you want, but you're not dining with me," she said.

"Why you chose to be with some teenage kid, who obviously doesn't care about you or she wouldn't have screwed your friend, instead of a real woman like me, I will never know," Helena huffed and walked down the hall towards her own room.

Graham sighed. "Come on," she said to Bailey. "You can wait for her in my room if you want."

Bailey followed her to the room a few doors down and sat down on the chair by the window after Graham opened the door. Graham sat on the edge of her bed, kicked her shoes off, and hung her throbbing head in her hands with her eyes closed. She tried rubbing her temples with her thumbs, but nothing was helping the intense pressure.

"How bad is it?" Bailey asked.

Graham could barely open her eyes to look at her.

"My mom used to get horrible migraines when I was little. My dad would put her head in his lap and massage her scalp until she fell asleep," Bailey said.

Graham nodded. "I don't think I've ever had a migraine. I very seldom get headaches especially like this, only when I'm stressed to my max."

"She used to describe it as feeling like your head was being squeezed in a vice and light or sound made it worse. I've never had one either," Bailey added.

"What did she do to make them stop?"

"She was an amazing woman, but they never stopped. She had a brain tumor and died when I was nine," Bailey said, wiping a few fresh tears from her face.

"Oh my god, I'm sorry, Bailey," Graham replied softly.

"Thanks."

"I've heard you mention your mom and dad. I didn't realize she was gone."

"That's Maggie, my step-mom. My dad remarried two years later. He had two small kids that needed more than he could provide alone. She's been a great second mom to me and my brother."

"You know all about my mom. She's definitely no cake walk, but it would be difficult if something like that happened to her especially if I were so young. How come you never told me?"

"I had planned to when I asked you to come home with me this summer and meet my family, but everything went to hell," Bailey said.

"You wanted me to meet your family?" Graham asked.

"I wanted to spend the rest of my life with you, Graham. I know I'm young and believe me that has been thrown in my face enough times, but I know I love you with all of my heart. I've never felt anything like I feel with you. People say you have your whole life ahead of you, well no one knows how long their whole life will be. My mom was thirty when she died."

"She was so young, but you do have your whole life ahead of you, Bailey. Whether it's ten years or seventy years, you're right we don't know. I'm graduating when we get back and you still have three more years here. So much is going to happen in your life during those three years. It's better that we move on now instead of when I leave. That will just make it harder in the long run. Neither of us expected to get serious so fast. If I've learned anything during my four years here it's that people come and go in your life and new experiences happen every year. That's what makes college so memorable." Graham tried to smiled.

"I disagree," Bailey said.

"Let's agree to disagree then and move on. We need to pull this team back together. It's the only way we are going to do what we set out to do at the beginning of the season and that's win a championship. That's why we are sitting where we are sitting right now."

"You and Dashtin need to work things out. She's your best friend, Graham. When I first met you both, I was jealous of her. When I realized you weren't together I was still jealous because of the bond the two of you share. Don't let all of this cause a river too wide to swim across between you. Like you said, you'll be leaving soon. I'm sure you're going separate your ways anyway.

Do you really want to go the rest of your life without your best friend?"

Graham smiled at her. "You're in the wrong major," she said.

Bailey laughed softly and stood up. "Eat an early dinner and take some ibuprofen. It will help your headache. Most of all, you need to sleep. Not eating or sleeping has taken its toll on you." She ran her hand through Graham's hair and walked out of the room.

Chapter 21

The next day, the Pioneers boarded the bus for the trip home. Wisconsin had lost their second game meaning the Pioneers were going to the Women's College World Series. They needed to get home quickly since they only had four days to prepare for the softball championship in Oklahoma.

Graham stared out the window for most of the long drive. Thankfully, no one sat next to her. She was ready to go home to her own bed. She tried to sleep but her mind kept drifting back to her conversation with Bailey. No matter how hard she tried to let her go, she kept finding a way to come right back into her life and invade her dreams. She closed her eyes and awoke again when she felt a hand on her shoulder. She opened her eyes to see Bailey standing there, smiling softly.

"We're back," she said.

"Thanks." Graham stretched and stood up.

Graham grabbed her bag when she got off the bus and headed straight for her Jeep. She drove home without looking back.

Dashtin arrived at the apartment close to an hour later after dropping off a few of their teammates. Graham was sitting on the couch when she walked in.

"Can we talk?" Graham said.

Dashtin nodded and sat down on the other end of the couch.

"For four years we've talked about going to the Women's College World Series and I always thought it would be a huge celebration and here we are going in a couple of days and we're not even speaking to each other. The team is falling apart. Everything is just one big mess."

"It's not how I envisioned it either," Dashtin said.

"Bailey and I talked yesterday."

"That's good."

"I'm not getting back with her. I care for her and you're right I do love her, but we both need to move on. She has so much time left here and with me graduating, my life is just beginning. She did bring up a good point though. She asked me if I wanted to go the rest of my life without my best friend," Graham said.

"What did you say?"

"I didn't say anything, but I thought about that entire conversation over and over in my head all night. Dashtin, I can't forgive what you did. Whether you intended to do it or not, you made a move on the one person in this world that meant everything to me. I will surely never forget it, and we may never go back to the way we were, but I do want you in my life."

"I don't expect you to forgive me either, but I don't want to lose our friendship. If it wasn't for you, I wouldn't be graduating in two weeks. I made the biggest mistake of my life purely by accident. I forgot who I was with and I let myself get caught up in a moment that wasn't even a moment. I've learned a lot from this. It's even made me question my career. If I can't be professional with my best friend's girlfriend, how can I be professional with strangers? I actually talked to one of my professors about it. He said that happens to everyone at least once during their career and not to worry about it. It's still on the back of my mind though."

"You're the only one that can make sure that fine line is always tight so you don't cross it," Graham said. "Worrying about that line is not a reason to give up what you worked so hard for."

"You're right. Just like you always are. I've missed having you to talk to these past few weeks. It sucks when the one person you need most won't talk to you."

"I know the feeling. It's not easy when that same person is also the reason you're upset or mad. I'm glad we're talking now, though," Graham said.

"Me too. Since we're talking, can I just say, I think it's a huge mistake for you to push Bailey away. You're clearly meant to be together."

"Sometimes things don't look as good on paper. Let's leave it at that," Graham said.

"I'm going out to get something to eat. Do you want to go?"

"No. I need to go check the mail and call my dad. I'm sure he saw the game last night and has already booked a plane to Oklahoma."

~

The next day, Graham walked into Coach Walker's office a few minutes before practice was supposed to start.

"Coach Walker, as the captain, I'd like to address the team before practice today," Graham said.

Coach Walker nodded. "I think that's a great idea. You look a little better than you did in Boise."

"I decided to start trying to right the sinking ship before it capsized." Graham walked into the locker room with Coach Walker behind her.

"Settle down, ladies. Your captain has something to say to you," Coach Walker said.

Graham waited for everyone to calm down and take a seat on one of the benches in front of the lockers.

"Let me be the first to apologize for the way my personal life has compromised this team over the past few weeks. Actions were made and words were said that indirectly effected everyone and as your captain, I'm sorry. We are on our way to the Women's College World Series for only the third time in school history. We should be celebrating and enjoying every minute of this and I for one am ready to get the party started in Oklahoma. I came to this school to play softball and win a championship. If you came here for the same reasons then let's put the past few weeks aside and play the game the way we know how!" Her voice rose in the last line.

Everyone clapped and cheered. They looked like the pumped up, excited team that they should be. Most of the girls high-fived Graham on their way out of the locker room for their practice session.

"I couldn't have said it better myself," Coach Walker said, patting Graham on the back as they took the field.

~

After a long plane ride, the Pioneers landed in Oklahoma City and waited for their luggage and equipment at the baggage claim station.

"I've never seen so many cowboy hats and pairs of boots in one place," Whitney said.

"I guess you've never been to Texas," Bailey said to her with a raised eyebrow. Whitney looked down at her tight jeans and boots realizing she fit right in.

"Country girls," Whitney said, shaking her head.

"What's that supposed to mean?" Bailey said.

"I've heard the saying there's nothing like a country girl. If you catch one, hang on for the ride," Whitney said.

Bailey laughed. "A country girl would rock your silly little world, city slicker."

Graham was listening to the two of them as she waited for the bags. She thought about commenting but knew better. Bailey did look smoking hot in her jeans and boots with her hair down in loose waves around her shoulders. For some reason, the worn-looking T-shirt with the Central Oregon logo stretched tightly across her chest didn't make her stand out. In fact, she seemed to fit right in with the locals, even taking the time to talk to a few people from other planes that were also waiting for their bags.

"She's a pistol, who knew?" Whitney said, nodding towards Bailey. Graham smiled, shaking her head.

Their bags began circling on the platform and everyone rushed to grab their own luggage as well as their batting bags. The coaches grabbed the rest of the team equipment and began loading everything onto large metal carts. Once they had everything, they pushed the carts outside to the large bus waiting along the curb that was similar to the ones they chartered for road trips. Each member of the team loaded her own bags and then helped load the remaining equipment.

Graham sat down next to Whitney at the front of the bus for the short ride through the city to the hotel.

"Are you okay sharing a room with Dashtin?" Whitney asked.

"Yeah, I'll be fine. We've talked and although things aren't exactly peachy keen, we do want to remain friends. Thanks for asking," Graham said. "In the end, we're all friends and we're all teammates. That's what's most important, next to winning the championship of course."

"Spoken like a true captain," Whitney teased.

Chapter 22

Graham was excited to take the field for their first game against Michigan, a team she'd never seen play. Bailey was pitching like a pro and the rest of the team was right on the money, scoring at least one run every inning. In the bottom of the sixth, Graham hit a two run RBI that took the Pioneers up over the other team by eight runs invoking the mercy rule and subsequently ending the game.

The next night, they played just as strongly against Virginia Tech, another team they'd never played. Whitney and Katie both hit home runs with runners on base and Sarah pitched the first three innings to give Bailey's arm some rest. She went two and a half innings with no hits and then the other team had found her weak spot and began getting hit after hit, so Bailey replaced her and closed out the game with mostly strikeouts before the other team could catch up to them on the scoreboard. The Pioneers shook hands with the other team and cheered all the way to their bus.

"What a game, ladies!" Coach Walker cheered with them as she stepped onto the bus. "If we keep playing like this we'll be unstoppable."

They arrived back at the hotel full of energy. The team was still cheering and celebrating their winning streak as they walked inside. Coach Walker and Coach Parker stayed outside with the bus driver, talking to him about their schedule for the next day.

Dashtin and Whitney went to check out the hotel bar while most of the team went into the dining room in search of late night snacks. It was already close to ten o'clock.

Graham continued to the elevator, shaking her head. She knew she was in for a long night with this group. Bailey jumped on before the doors closed.

"You pitched a great game today," Graham said.

"Thanks. Everyone is playing so well."

The doors opened on their floor and they went to their separate rooms. Graham looked back over her shoulder in time to see Bailey enter her room. She opened her own door and went straight to the shower. The hot water helped relax her aching muscles. Squatting to catch a ball for the past eight years was starting to catch up to her. She finished her shower and barely had time to cover up with a towel before Dashtin barged into the bathroom like her hair was on fire.

"What's wrong?" Graham asked, pulling her towel a little tighter.

"Get dressed. We're all meeting in twenty minutes and going to that honky-tonk bar downstairs," Dashtin said, stripping her uniform and turning the shower on.

Graham shook her head and walked out of the bathroom before Dashtin was completely naked.

Graham dressed in a relaxed fit pair of jeans and a black T-shirt. She searched her bag for suitable footwear and was thankful she'd decided to pack her Doc Marten's. She was sure flip flops or sneakers weren't proper attire for a honky-tonk in the middle of Oklahoma. She put a little bit of gel in her messy short hair and sat in the chair by the window to tie her shoes.

Dashtin emerged from the bathroom a few minutes later with her long hair freshly blow-dried. Graham had no idea how she could shower and dry her hair in record time, but she seemed to do it like it was second nature. Graham watched her pull on a pair of jeans, a polo shirt with the collar wide open, and a dark pair of shoes.

"Ready?" Dashtin said.

Graham nodded and followed Dashtin out of the room. As angry as she was with her best friend over the few weeks, she was happy to have her back in her life. Most of the girls were also in the hallway. Graham saw Bailey talking to Whitney. Her hair was down around her shoulders and curlier than normal because she didn't have time to blow-dry it. She looked like the country girl that she was in boots, tight jeans, and a tight T-shirt stretched across her breasts that was short enough for the silky tan skin of her stomach to peak out when she moved a certain way. She was sexy; there was no doubt about it. Graham looked away.

Country music was blaring when they stepped out of the elevator. Dashtin led the group into the bar. She and Whitney pulled a bunch of high-top tables together and the rest of the girls gathered around. Graham looked around and there were a lot of local people and at least two other softball teams in the small bar. The dance floor was packed with people line dancing.

The waitress carded everyone and brought a couple of pitchers of light beer out to the handful that were old enough to drink. She filled their plastic cups to the top for the first round. The rest of the group ordered sodas. Dashtin held her beer up to toast the team after all of the drinks arrived. It had been a while since Graham had gone and the cold beer rushing down her throat tasted better than ever.

A few of the girls disappeared to the dance floor. Bailey squeezed right into the front of the line dancing group and began moving right along with them. Graham leaned against the table watching Bailey dance. Katie and Sarah were in the back trying to figure out the dance and had just gotten the steps down when the song was over. Another fast song started and the group began dancing a completely different line dance that apparently Bailey knew all of the steps to. She hooked her thumbs through her belt loops and spun around kicking and clapping in step with everyone around her.

"No matter how hard I try, I can't do that shit," Katie said breathlessly.

Dashtin laughed. "Don't look at me. I'm from Seattle."

The next song broke the group up into couples dancing along to the fast song. Whitney and Vanessa raced out to the floor to shake it with Bailey. They were smiling and laughing together as they danced. A bunch of players from the other two teams were also out there dancing.

"Want to join them?" Dashtin asked Graham.

"I'm scared to get into that crowd." Graham laughed.

"Oh come on," Dashtin pushed her towards the wooden floor. They danced together, but kept their distance.

The next song started and Bailey grabbed the front of Graham's shirt, pulling her close. Graham looked down, shaking her head no. Bailey grinned and moved against her. Dashtin and Whitney both raised an eyebrow and watched the younger woman work her magic, teasing Graham as she rocked her hips back and forth. It took seconds for Graham to react. She wrapped her arms around Bailey's slender waist grinding their bodies together. She bent Bailey back with their crotches together and pulled her back up against her. They moved seductively like a scene from the movie 'Dirty Dancing', but stayed right on the beat of the fast country song.

Graham stepped away from Bailey, walking back to the table as the song changed to a slower one. She drank a long sip of her cold beer.

"I never knew country music could be that hot," Whitney teased, stepping up to the table next to Graham.

Graham rolled her eyes taking another sip.

"Maybe I can find a little country girl to rock my world while we're here," Whitney said, eyeing the crowd. "Who's that with Bailey?"

Graham turned to see Bailey standing near the dance floor with her arms around a girl that was a little bit taller than her with light brown hair. They looked a little too close for a friendly hug.

"I have no idea," Graham said. "Maybe she has a new girlfriend."

178

"It looked to me like you two were back together," Whitney said.

"We're not," Graham said.

The music changed again to a faster song and Bailey walked back to the dance floor with the mystery girl.

"It looks like they definitely know each other," Whitney said, watching the two girls dancing closely. Bailey kept her distance, not exactly grinding with the girl like she had done with Graham, but the girl tried hard to get closer to her.

Graham grabbed Whitney's hand and pulled her to the dance floor. They'd rarely danced together, but Whitney fell right into step moving against Graham until she was tapped on the shoulder by a busty blond in short shorts and cowboy boots. Whitney laughed and backed away allowing the Daisy Duke look-a-like to step into Graham's dance space.

Graham danced close to the stranger who made it a point to rub her large fake boobs on her. She was very pretty and by the way she was dancing on Graham like she was a human pole, Graham figured she was probably a dancer at a local gentleman's club. She moved to the beat of the music matching every roll of the blonde's flirtatious hips with her own until the blond was replaced by a petite brunette with daggers in her green eyes.

The song changed and everyone on the floor separated for another line dance. Graham walked back to the table with Bailey hot on her heels.

"Where's the blond?" Dashtin asked.

"Daisy Duke needed to get her ass back to Hazard County," Bailey sneered.

"Who are you to say anything?" Graham looked at her.

Bailey was about to put her in her place when the stranger she had been seen dancing with walked up casually placing her arm around Bailey's shoulders. Graham raised an eyebrow. Bailey slid away from the embrace.

"And you are?" Dashtin asked.

"Sammy," the girl said, sticking her hand out.

"As in-" Graham started.

"Yes," Bailey answered. "She plays for Texas A&M."

"What a nice time for a reunion. It looks like you two are catching up right where you left off. Don't let me get in the way," Graham said sarcastically, reaching for the pitcher to refill her cup.

"I'm sorry I chased off your bimbo. Would you like me to go down the street to the titty bar and bring her back?" Bailey growled.

Graham shook her head and grinned. She tried to walk away but Bailey stopped her near the table.

"You've got a thing or two to learn about me if you think I'm going to let you mess around on me twice," Graham said.

"I wasn't out there rubbing all over some nasty stripper!"

"No, you were just grinding all over your ex-girlfriend because that's so much better," Graham countered and walked towards the dance floor.

"How long have they been together?" Sammy asked, listening to the heated conversation a few feet away.

180

"A while," Dashtin said eyeing the stranger. She was obviously Bailey's age and pretty with light brown hair and brown eyes. "How do you know Bailey?"

"We're from the same town. We went to school together," Sammy said, watching Bailey follow Graham to the middle of the room.

The fast song ended and a slow song began.

"Dance with me," Bailey said, pulling Graham into her arms.

"Bailey," Graham chided, shaking her head.

"One dance and I'll go my own way for the rest of the night if that's what you want," Bailey added, placing her arms around Graham's neck. Graham gave in, wrapping her arms around Bailey's waist, keeping space between them.

They swayed back and forth, slowly closing the gap as the song progressed. Bailey laid her head on Graham's shoulder, facing her neck. Graham closed her eyes. Holding Bailey against her felt so good. The scent of her floral shampoo sent chills down her spine. She missed the way Bailey felt in her arms.

They pulled away from each other slowly when the song ended. Bailey reached up to wipe tears from her face, but Graham's hand was already there. She looked up into blue eyes as Graham caught the tears, pushing them aside gently with her thumb.

"I'm tired of pretending I don't love you," Graham said, bending her head and softly kissing Bailey's lips.

Bailey opened her mouth to Graham deepening the kiss. She wrapped her arms around her as tears of sadness turned to tears of joy. An eruption of cheers broke their concentration. Graham and Bailey turned to see all of their teammates cheering for them. Graham wrapped her arm around Bailey walking back to the table with a huge smile on her face.

"It's about time you two figured it out," Whitney said, holding her cup in the air.

"I think I'm going to call it a night," Graham said. "No more beer and don't stay here too much longer. We have a big day tomorrow and everyone needs to be fresh on their feet without foggy heads."

Bailey grabbed Graham's hand, walking out of the bar with her. They rode the elevator up to the fourth floor and stepped off together.

"I want to take it slow. Is that okay with you?" Graham said.

"Nothing matters as long as I have you," Bailey said.

Graham kissed her a little harder than she meant to, pushing Bailey back against the wall. Bailey ran her hands up Graham's back under her shirt. Both women pulled away breathless.

"So much for going slow," Bailey teased.

Graham grinned. "Goodnight. I'll see you in the morning," she said before walking to her room.

Chapter 23

The next afternoon, Graham was late meeting the team for lunch and no one had seen her all morning because her socialite mother had her doing a phone interview for her high-society newspaper. She didn't want to do the interview, but she didn't feel like dealing with the wrath of her mother who was apparently way too busy with her social calendar to fly to Oklahoma to actually see her daughter play.

Graham had just stepped from the elevator when she ran into Sammy coming out of the dining room.

"You'd be surprised what a stroll down memory lane does to the mind," Sammy said.

"What are you getting at?"

"Bailey's already talking about getting together when she comes home for the summer in a few weeks."

"Is that so? Let me tell you something, Sammy. If you want to be in Bailey's life you'd better get used to my name and used to seeing me around because I'm not going anywhere," Graham said, stepping a little closer.

183

"You never forget your first love, just remember that," Sammy snickered and walked away.

Graham shook her head and walked into the dining room. Bailey was sitting with Claudia and Katie.

"What's the matter, Graham? Country girl rock your world a little too hard?" Whitney said.

Graham rolled her eyes and flipped her the bird as she walked towards the breakfast bar. She methodically placed a turkey sandwich, a spoonful of macaroni and cheese, and a banana on her plate and sat down next to Dashtin across from Whitney.

Whitney opened her mouth to speak and Graham picked up her banana pointing it at her.

"If you say one more stupid remark I'm going to slap you with this," Graham said.

"That bad?" Dashtin said.

"I swear the woman thinks she's a Kennedy and she's more like the 'unsinkable Molly Brown' from the Titanic," Graham said.

"I can't believe your mom made you do a phone interview for her newspaper," Whitney said.

Graham looked at Dashtin. "Everyone kept asking where you were since Bailey was here and not with you. I said you were talking with your mother's newspaper."

"It's not actually my mother's paper. It's more of a high-society newsletter for the people of Oregon who think their shit doesn't stink. My mother's a pain in my ass," Graham said between bites of her sandwich.

"I meant to tell you, my dad finally made it. He was able to get out of going to Tokyo," Dashtin said.

"Oh that's great that he made it for the finals," Graham said.

"I can't believe the hometown favorite, Oklahoma, lost in the late game last night and now we're in the finals against Texas A&M for the championship," Whitney said.

"I personally wish we were playing someone else," Graham said, opening her banana.

"How did the thing go with your mom?" Bailey asked, taking a bite of Graham's banana from her hand as she stood next to her.

Graham looked up at her and smiled. "Fine. I'm sure my interview will be on the front page," she said, pushing her chair back to go clear her plate in the trash. "I ran into your old flame in the hallway before I came in here. She made some comment about hooking up when you go home for the summer."

"Oh good grief," Bailey rolled her eyes. "Sammy's just trying to push your buttons. She can be an ass sometimes. I said we should get together for lunch one day to catch up when I'm home."

Graham grinned. "I think I told her something along the lines of get used to me because I'm not going anywhere."

Bailey kissed her cheek. "You have nothing to worry about. In fact, I may have added fuel to the fire the other night when I told her I was madly in love with you and planned to spend the rest of my life with you. That's why she came over and put her arm around me."

"I need your attention, ladies. We have a few hours before the game tonight and I want everyone to be in conference room 2B in an hour to watch some film and go over our strategy," Coach Walker said to the group.

"Film, oh what fun," Dashtin said sarcastically as Coach Walker left the room.

Bailey and Graham laughed.

"There goes my plans for the next few hours," Bailey said, grinning at Graham.

~

Watching the film, Graham learned two valuable things. The first was that the other team was a heavy swinging team, meaning they often swung at every pitch which could work in her and Bailey's favor. The second being Sammy was a base stealer which meant she now had two targets on her back where Graham was concerned.

After the films, everyone retired to their rooms to get ready for the bus ride over to the stadium. They were labeled as the home team for the game so Graham dressed in her white uniform with the word Pioneers written across her chest in light blue with a black outline.

"Are you ready for this?" Dashtin said to her.

"I've been waiting four years to step onto that field in the finals of the championship. I'm glad we're doing this together," she said.

"Me too. Let's go kick some ass," Dashtin yelled.

Chapter 24

Game one of the Women's College World Series got underway quickly. It was a best of three series making each game count. The Pioneers pulled off a three to one win with careful pitching and unbelievable defense. Katie hit a home run and Claudia hit a two-run RBI in the sixth inning and Bailey struck out all three batters in the final inning.

Everyone was so tired from the long day that they pretty much all collapsed in their beds when they got back to the hotel. Bailey spent a little extra time in the hallway kissing Graham goodnight.

"I wish I was sleeping in your bed next to you tonight," Bailey said.

Graham grinned and kissed her lips. "You and I don't seem to get much sleep when we're in the same bed," she said.

"That's true and I'm so tired right now I'd probably fall asleep before I got all of my clothes off," Bailey said, pulling Graham in for another kiss before parting ways.

~

The next night, the Pioneers arrived at the stadium for game two of the series with a one to nothing lead. They would win the championship if they were able to win this next game.

Texas A&M was up first. Graham called the pitches and Bailey threw the ball perfectly every time, striking out the first two girls easily. The next batter stepped purposefully close to Graham as she entered the box.

"I wouldn't get so comfortable if I were you," Sammy said, adjusting her hands on the bat.

"I could say the same thing," Graham replied, giving the signal for the pitch.

She knew that Sammy was familiar with all of Bailey's pitches after watching her hit the day before, but Bailey's ball control had improved tremendously since the start of the season. She called a screwball which used to be Bailey's worst pitch and sat back to catch the ball as it whizzed past Sammy's swinging bat. The next pitch was an off speed rise ball that Sammy swung at too early. Graham smiled and called the third pitch. Bailey threw the ball and watched it curve inside at just the right time nearly hitting Sammy. The goal was to get her to check her swing too far and she did just that. When the ball came too close the bat came around behind it.

Graham laughed as Sammy walked away visibly angry. She caught up to Bailey, putting her arm around her as they walked into the dugout.

"She's pissed," Bailey said. "I've never struck her out."

"Good." Graham grinned.

The rest of the game went the same way with both sides struggling at the plate until Graham hit a ground ball to third in the fifth inning with one out. She ran as fast as she could to first base and was hit in the back by the ball because of a crazy throw to first by Sammy who happened to be playing third base. The hit knocked the wind out of Graham and she fell into the first baseman.

Coach Walker immediately ran out of the dugout, shouting at the umpire who called her out.

"That was an intentional hit and you damn well know it," she shouted.

Graham was still sitting on the ground trying to catch her breath as Coach Parker knelt down beside her.

"I'm okay," Graham said, standing up. She waved to her father in stands so he would know she was alright.

"That didn't look like an accident to me," Coach Parker said as they walked back to the dugout together.

"It wasn't," Graham said. "That bitch on third base is Bailey's ex-girlfriend from high school."

"What are you going to do about this?" Coach Parker asked.

"We're going to win this damn championship."

"Good, go relay that message to your team so they don't retaliate," Coach Parker patted her shoulder and went over to Coach Walker who was still yelling at the umpire and the other team's coach near the plate.

Bailey ran up to Graham as soon as she neared the dugout. "She's aggressive. I should've warned you. Are you okay?"

"I'm fine," Graham said, pulling all of the girls together. "Don't worry about that crazy bitch. We're here to win a game and win it legally. Do you remember when Washington cheated and gave us our first loss of the season? We don't want to be like them, cheating to win," she said. Everyone high-fived and cheered, "Pioneers". Graham turned to Dashtin who had come in from the plate to make sure her best friend was okay. "Dashtin, you're up next. Swing low enough to get under one of those drop ball pitches and you might be able to hit it to the parking lot."

Dashtin nodded and walked to the plate. She watched the first pitch rise high out of the strike zone. She set her feet and bent her knees as the ball left the pitchers hand. She watched it sink lower and lower as she brought the bat around. A loud crack was heard as the bat connected with the ball, pushing it deep across the field.

Dashtin was just about to cross first base as the ball cleared the outfield fence. She threw her arms up and trotted past second. She slowed down when she got to third.

"It takes a real loser to get ahead by hurting someone," Dashtin said as she stepped on the bag and turned for home.

The entire Pioneer team was waiting at home plate jumping up and down, cheering for her. She walked into the middle of the group, stomping on the plate and yelling with her arms over her head. The coaches cheered and ushered the group back into the dugout. Katie batted next hitting a pop-up all the way to the fence that centerfielder caught, diving through the grass for the last out

The sixth inning had been hitless for both teams as the Pioneers took the field for the top of the seventh inning. All they needed was three outs to end the game and win the championship. The top of the Texas A&M lineup was coming to the plate.

"Three up and three down," Graham said, smiling at Bailey before they parted on the field.

The first batter hit a pop-up for the first out and the next batter struck out, bringing Sammy to the plate. She hit a ground ball that slipped past the third base player and Dashtin ran after it but Sammy was already safe at first base before she was able to throw it over.

Graham grinned. She had been waiting for this moment after seeing the film on the Texas team and learning that Sammy was their number one base stealer. She gave Bailey the steal signal as the next batter stepped into the box.

Bailey turned around and winked at Sammy before pitching the ball then diving to the ground as Graham caught it and launched it to second base in time for Vanessa to tag Sammy as she slid past the plate.

The umpire jumped up shouting, "Out!"

The Texas coach went crazy, yelling at the umpire as Graham tore off her mask and ran to Bailey, picking her up in the middle of the field. The rest of the team crowded around them, falling to the ground in a huge pile of white uniforms, screaming and yelling with joy.

The umpire called the end of the game, ignoring the complaints from the Texas A&M coach and declared the Pioneers the winners and champions.

"I love you so damn much," Graham said to Bailey at the bottom of the pile. She had the biggest smile that Bailey had ever seen on her face.

"I love you too," Bailey said, kissing her.

The group of players shifted and maneuvered until they were no longer a pile, revealing their catcher and pitcher lying in the dirt, locked in an embrace for the entire crowd to see. Bailey quickly jumped off of Graham and stood up. Graham laughed and got to her feet as well. Everyone rushed to the plate for the proverbial slapping of hands with the losing team before cheering and jumping up and down once again.

Dashtin and Whitney picked up Coach Walker on their shoulders and Graham and Sarah did the same with Coach Parker as they celebrated in front of home plate.

"You girls are amazing," Coach Walker shouted when the coaches were put back on their feet. "What a season!"

The championship trophy was presented to Graham as the captain of the team. She kissed the side of it and handed to Bailey who kissed it too. Graham and Dashtin picked Bailey up on their shoulders as she hailed the trophy over her head.

The parents in the stands rushed to the field to join the celebration when they put Bailey down and began passing the trophy around to each member of the team. Graham's father hugged her tightly.

"I'm so damn proud of you," he said. "With this and with school. Why didn't you call me you when you got the graduate school letter?"

"Thanks, dad. I was waiting to tell you in person. I didn't think mom would have her little news thing sent to you." she said.

"She does crap like that to rub things in my face. Either way, I'm very happy for you."

"Graham," Bailey called from a few feet away, waving Graham over to her. Bailey was standing with a man that looked a lot like Tim McGraw with dark facial hair, a Pioneer baseball cap, jeans, and cowboy boots. He had his arm around the woman next to him with her reddish brown hair pulled back in a ponytail. She was also wearing jeans and boots.

"I'll be right back, dad. There's someone I want you to meet," Graham said, walking over to the group that was staring at her.

Bailey grabbed her hand. "Everyone, this is Graham Cahill, my girlfriend. Graham this is the Michaels family. My dad, Calvin, my mom, Sonya and my brother, Calvin Junior," Bailey said.

Graham shook hands with each of them.

"You've been keeping a huge secret little lady," Sonya said to Bailey and gave her a thumbs up.

"What are your intentions with my daughter?" Calvin said.

"Daddy," Bailey warned.

"No, Bailey, it's okay. Sir, I'm graduating with my Bachelor of Science Degree in Biology this coming weekend and I've been accepted back to UCO to complete my Master's this fall in Microbiology. So, if Bailey loves me as much as I love her, I would like her to move in with me. I intend to never let her go again," Graham said.

"You didn't tell me you got accepted," Bailey said.

"With everything going on recently I sort of put it aside," Graham said with a shrug.

"I'm happy for you and I can't wait to move in with you," Bailey said, smiling up at her.

"Welcome to the family, Graham. We expect to see you with Bailey when she comes home for the summer," Calvin said to her.

"I would like nothing more, Sir, but first, I want to go spend some time with my father. Bailey, there's someone I would like you to meet," Graham said, waving her dad over. "This is my father, Edward Cahill. Dad, this is my girlfriend, Bailey Michaels and her family."

Everyone shook hands and introduced themselves. Within minutes, they'd decided to take the girls out for a celebratory dinner.

"I think that went well," Bailey said, squeezing her hand.

"Me too." Graham smiled, pulling Bailey away from their parents.

"I don't think I've ever been happier than I am right now, Graham. I love you so much."

"I love you too, Bailey," Graham said.

"Hey, your dad just told me that you were accepted for grad school, Graham. That's awesome," Dashtin said, walking up to them. "I actually have some news of my own. Upon graduation, you're looking at the new assistant athletic trainer for the Seattle Storm WNBA team."

"No way! That's great, Dash. I knew you interviewed with them over the holidays, but you never said anything else," Graham said, hugging her best friend.

"I hadn't heard anything from them until I got the call a couple days ago and honestly it hasn't really sunk in yet."

"There are going to be a lot of broken hearted basketball players," Bailey teased.

Dashtin laughed. "I don't know. Maybe someday when I'm old and gray I will find what you guys have."

"Good luck with that." Graham smiled.

"Are you ladies ready to go to dinner?" Graham's father said. "Dashtin, you're welcome to join us."

"Thank you, Mr. Cahill, but my dad's here so I think we're going to dinner," Dashtin said.

"Well, invite him along. The more the merrier. We're all family here," he said to her.

"He's right, Dash. We are family, all of us," Graham said.

About the Author

Graysen Morgen was born and raised in North Florida with winding rivers and waterways at her back door and the white sandy beach a mile away. She has spent most of her lifetime in the sun and on the water. She enjoys reading, writing, fishing, and spending as much time as possible with her partner and their daughter.

You can contact Graysen at graysenmorgen@aol.com and like her fan page on facebook.com/graysenmorgen.

Go to www.tri-pub.com to get information about Triplicity Publishing or to submit your own manuscript.

Other Titles Available From

Triplicity Publishing

Falling Snow by Graysen Morgen. Dr. Cason Macauley, a high-speed trauma surgeon from Denver meets Adler Troy, a professional snowboarder and sparks fly. The last thing Cason wants is a relationship and Adler doesn't realize what's right in front of her until it's gone, but will it be too late?

Fate vs. Destiny by Graysen Morgen. Logan Greer devotes her life to investigating plane crashes for the National Transportation Safety Board. Brooke McCabe is an investigator with the Federal Aviation Association who literally flies by the seat of her pants. When Logan gets tangled in head games with both women will she choose fate or destiny?

Just Me by Graysen Morgen. Wild child Ian Wiley has to grow up and take the reins of the hundred year old family business when tragedy strikes. Cassidy Harland is a little surprised that she came within an inch of picking up a gorgeous stranger in a bar and is shocked to find out that stranger is the new head of her company.

Love Loss Revenge by Graysen Morgen. Rian Casey is an FBI Agent working the biggest case of her career and madly in love with her girlfriend. Her world is turned upside when tragedy strikes. Heartbroken, she tries to rebuild her life. When she discovers the truth behind what really happened that awful night she decides justice isn't good enough, and vows revenge on everyone involved.

Natural Instinct by Graysen Morgen. Chandler Scott is a Marine Biologist who keeps her private life private. Corey Joslen is intrigued by Chandler from the moment she meets her. Chandler is forced to finally open her life up to Corey. It backfires in Corey's face and sends her running. Will either woman learn to trust her natural instinct?

Secluded Heart by Graysen Morgen. Chase Leery is an overworked cardiac surgeon with a group of best friends that have an opinion and a reason for everything. When she meets a new artist named Remy Sheridan at her best friend's art gallery she is captivated by the reclusive woman. When Chase finds out why Remy is so sheltered will she put her career on the line to help her or is it too difficult to love someone with a secluded heart?

In Love, at War by Graysen Morgen. Charley Hayes is in the Army Air Force and stationed at Ford Island in Pearl Harbor. She is the commanding officer of her own female-only service squadron and doing the one thing she loves most, repairing airplanes. Life is good for Charley, until the day she finds herself falling in love while fighting for her life as her country is thrown haphazardly into World War II. Can she survive being in love and at war?

Submerged by Graysen Morgen. Assistant District Attorney Layne Carmichael had no idea that the sexy woman she took home from a local bar for a one night stand would turn out to be someone she would be prosecuting months later. Scooter is a Naval Officer on a submarine who changes women like she changes uniforms. When she is accused of a heinous crime she is shocked to see her latest conquest sitting across from her as the prosecuting attorney.

Bridesmaid of Honor by Graysen Morgen. Britton Prescott's best friend is getting married and she's the maid of honor. What her best friend failed to mention, was the fact that her cousin Daphne was going to be a bridesmaid. The same cousin who has been Britton's nemesis since they were in high school. Everyone is counting on Britton and Daphne to behave like adults and put the past behind them. No one expects to find them wrapped in each other's arms at the most inopportune time.

Vow of Solitude by Austen Thorne. Detective Jordan Denali is in a fight for her life against the ghosts from her past and a Serial Killer taunting her with his every move. She lives a life of solitude and plans to keep it that way. When Callie Marceau, a curious Medical Examiner, decides she wants in on the biggest case of her career, as well as, Jordan's life, Jordan is powerless to stop her.

Igniting Temptation by Sydney Canyon. Mackenzie Trotter is the Head of Pediatrics at the local hospital. Her life takes a rather unexpected turn when she meets a flirtatious, beautiful fire fighter. Both women soon discover it doesn't take much to ignite temptation.

One Night by Sydney Canyon. While on a business trip, Caylen Jarrett spends an amazing night with a beautiful stripper. Months later, she is shocked and confused when that same woman re-enters her life. The fact that this stranger could destroy her career doesn't bother her. C.J. is more terrified of the feelings this woman stirs in her. Could she have fallen in love in one night and not even known it?